not like normal

(an ilse beck fbi suspense thriller—book 7)

ava strong

Ava Strong

Bestselling author Ava Strong is author of the REMI LAURENT mystery series, comprising six books (and counting); of the ILSE BECK mystery series, comprising seven books (and counting); of the STELLA FALL psychological suspense thriller series, comprising six books (and counting); and of the DAKOTA STEELE FBI suspense thriller series, comprising three books (and counting).

An avid reader and lifelong fan of the mystery and thriller genres, Ava loves to hear from you, so please feel free to visit www.avastrongauthor.com to learn more and stay in touch.

Copyright © 2022 by Ava Strong. All rights reserved. Except as permitted under the U.S. Copyright Act of 1976, no part of this publication may be reproduced, distributed or transmitted in any form or by any means, or stored in a database or retrieval system, without the prior permission of the author. This ebook is licensed for your personal enjoyment only. This ebook may not be re-sold or given away to other people. If you would like to share this book with another person, please purchase an additional copy for each recipient. If you're reading this book and did not purchase it, or it was not purchased for your use only, then please return it and purchase your own copy. Thank you for respecting the hard work of this author. This is a work of fiction. Names, characters, businesses, organizations, places, events, and incidents either are the product of the author's imagination or are used fictionally. Any resemblance to actual persons, living or dead, is entirely coincidental. Jacket image Copyright Dinca Maria Mihaela, used under license from Shutterstock.com.
ISBN: 978-1-0943-9540-1

BOOKS BY AVA STRONG

REMI LAURENT FBI SUSPENSE THRILLER
THE DEATH CODE (Book #1)
THE MURDER CODE (Book #2)
THE MALICE CODE (Book #3)
THE VENGEANCE CODE (Book #4)
THE DECEPTION CODE (Book #5)
THE SEDUCTION CODE (Book #6)

ILSE BECK FBI SUSPENSE THRILLER
NOT LIKE US (Book #1)
NOT LIKE HE SEEMED (Book #2)
NOT LIKE YESTERDAY (Book #3)
NOT LIKE THIS (Book #4)
NOT LIKE SHE THOUGHT (Book #5)
NOT LIKE BEFORE (Book #6)
NOT LIKE NORMAL (Book #7)

STELLA FALL PSYCHOLOGICAL SUSPENSE THRILLER
HIS OTHER WIFE (Book #1)
HIS OTHER LIE (Book #2)
HIS OTHER SECRET (Book #3)
HIS OTHER MISTRESS (Book #4)
HIS OTHER LIFE (Book #5)
HIS OTHER TRUTH (Book #6)

DAKOTA STEELE FBI SUSPENSE THRILLER
WITHOUT MERCY (Book #1)
WITHOUT REMORSE (Book #2)
WITHOUT A PAST (Book #3)

PROLOGUE

Erin's eyes fluttered, and she wondered where she was. Flickers of sunlight jabbed like needles while dark spots faded from her gaze. Her eyelids moved slow, heavy.

She tried to sit up, but realize she couldn't move her arms.

A slow, cold panic set in. She tried to shift, tried to kick, but her legs didn't work either.

The panic blossomed into outright terror.

Where was she? Why could she barely open her eyes?

And that's when she heard the faint whir of wheels. She couldn't move, but she could feel. And now, she felt her body jouncing and swaying with the sound of wheels.

At last, her eyes opened.

She found her head downturned, staring at her legs. And past her shifting feet, she spotted a neatly arranged cobblestone pathway—red and blue and gray bricks patterned in symmetrical displays.

She watched her legs shift and sway, directed by the motion of the…

Wheelchair? She was in a wheelchair.

The terror trembled down her spine, now. The fear threatened to constrict her throat. She tried to speak, to protest, but her lips barely moved. She could feel the way her lips touched against each other, feeling as if someone had swabbed cotton through her dry mouth. She swallowed, but even this with great difficulty. And then she realized someone was behind her. She could hear him whistling, a merry tune. He continued to push her, guiding the wheelchair up the cobblestone path.

Off to the right, she heard someone say, "Good morning!"

The faint whistling sound continued, suggesting that whoever was wheeling her forward didn't return the greeting.

She detected the faint scent of coffee. The odor of freshly baked dough. The sunlight and random greeting suggested it was daytime. So why couldn't she remember last night?

She tried to move again. But it was as if her muscles had all disconnected from her brain.

Had she been injured? Was she at a hospital?

The voice behind her was whistling still. Every now and then, out of the corner of her eye, she spotted figures moving past. Then she recognized the location: an open air shopping center she had often frequented herself.

Why was she here? Why couldn't she move?

She tried to scream, but again her lips didn't so much as flinch.

She realized now that she was being pushed up an incline.

The cobblestone turned to gray asphalt. She was now in a multilevel parking lot. How many times had she come through the same spot herself? She would often visit, during the summers, to grab an orange mango smoothie from the small coffee shop on the corner.

As they entered the parking structure, she felt more chills down her spine. But there was absolutely nothing she could do. The scent of coffee and baked goods was replaced by fuel and rubber.

The man behind her continued to wheel her forward. They turned once, twice, heading towards the top of the structure.

Why wasn't he talking? Why wasn't he saying anything?

She needed help. She needed to scream. Something was wrong. She wasn't at a hospital. She could barely remember the previous night, but it was starting to come back. She had been in her bed; everything had been fine.

And then the sound of shattered glass.

Someone had broken into her home. And now, here she was.

The panic flared.

The whistling behind her stopped. The wheels continued to whir. Her hair shifted in front of her face as the jostling motion sent her leaning forward.

Gray hair. Silver bangs.

Stunned, she stared. She didn't have silver hair—her hair was blonde.

Were her eyes playing tricks?

Suddenly, she felt two clicking sensations. The man behind her was adjusting something on the wheelchair. She found the seat slowly shifting up, and she nearly slid off.

She could feel the wind, could feel the breeze and the sunlight against her skin. Could feel the sweat prickling her forehead. The odor of the parking lot, and of the open air mall all faded. And now, she stared in horror, as her wheelchair was slowly pushed towards the edge of the parking lot. They were three stories up. There was an opening, for construction—an intended expansion. The caution tape was brushed aside. A small, orange traffic cone toppled. The man behind her was wheeling her towards the edge of the roof. Faster, faster. They picked up speed. The wheels spun.

She wanted to scream, but there was absolutely nothing she could do.

CHAPTER ONE

Ilse's sense of discomfort had reached new heights. She fidgeted uncomfortably in front of her dinosaur of a computer, staring at the screen as the slow connection of her equally slow processor finally displayed the webpage.

How often had Sawyer tried to convince her to get a new laptop? She had refused on principle. But now, she was reaping the reward for her stiffnecked determination.

Ilse shifted, reading the text on the screen. Behind her, from her wood-burning stove, she detected the faint scent of cinnamon. A new batch of granola. Homemade. Something she hadn't done since she had moved from her lake house. But she was determined to get back to the things she enjoyed. Things that made her life unique to her.

Because she was just so damn tired of allowing her father to dictate her mood.

But even with the faint scent of the cinnamon granola, and the quiet tick of the analog clock over her stove, nothing could help curb the rising sense of frustration as she read the report on her screen.

He wasn't doing *anything*.

"What are you playing at?" She murmured to herself. Her fingers brushed the side of her face, sending some of her hair over her injured ear. The ear had been a gift from her father. Along with years of trauma.

And now, after nearly twenty years, Gerald Mueller was being released from prison.

He had been granted parole, and was now living in a small, single story house that he had rented with money he shouldn't have had. This wasn't the part that surprised Ilse. She knew her father had connections on the outside. What bothered her most was how he seemed to be just sitting there. Waiting. Watching television. Eating food he ordered over the Internet.

Why wasn't he doing anything? Where was his female accomplice?

Ilse's frustration was palpable.

Gerald Mueller, a man who had stolen so much of her innocence, was pretending as if he wasn't a sadistic killer.

And while Ilse didn't like the idea of using her FBI credentials to keep track of a personal case, she had pulled some strings. BKA, German feds, had been willing to give her updates on her father, in exchange for an interview about him. There wasn't much she had been able to tell them they didn't already know.

Some of the more personal things, from her family, she had left unsaid.

"Where is she?" Ilse murmured. "Come on," she snapped, slapping a hand against the table.

The webpage had frozen, failing to load completely.

With a frustrated sigh, she wiggled with some of the cables behind her desktop.

She could feel her temper rising. She settled, inhaling slowly. She closed her eyes, using one of the breathing tricks she so often taught her clients.

In, out. A pause.

She inhaled the faint scent of cinnamon. Things were improving in her life. She couldn't afford to think otherwise. Her father was under surveillance. Whoever had been sending her those taunting postcards for months had finally stopped.

She hadn't seen another postcard nor tchotchke in her mail. There was no reason to let her anxiety get the better of her.

The analog clock, the desktop computer as old as some teenagers, and her wood-burning stove were all testament to her hatred of all things technology. But the direction society was heading meant that Ilse was going to have to make a tough decision sooner or later. Many of her clients were starting to prefer online meetings. She cared too much about helping the survivors of men like her father to not at least consider updating her device.

"One thing at a time," she said out loud. Ilse had a ticket to Germany next week. But five days was a long time to wait. Especially because the BKA reports yielded nothing. What was her father playing at? Was he planning something? Was he just taunting them in his inaction?

It didn't feel right that he was allowed to go free. Ilse hadn't managed to make his parole, though.

She'd had something more important to tend to.

Her mind moved to agent Tom Sawyer. In her imagination, she glimpsed his stubborn, green eyes. The scent of sandalwood aftershave and sawdust. His flannel shirts, his baseball cap. His sandy hair, and thin frame.

Now, though, the picture had other memories. Sawyer crying. His rage.

He was exactly the sort of person she helped in her counseling. But a few days ago, it wasn't counseling he had needed. It was a rescuer. She had saved him from himself.

She shivered, remembering the sheer loathing in his gaze. Tom Sawyer had gone into a federal prison with the intent of murdering the man who had killed his sister. Ilse had gotten there just in time. She felt a strange mixture of emotions while thinking of Sawyer... She frowned, trying to stave off a rising sense of... sympathy? Affection? She wanted to call him... in a way, she was almost glad she had an excuse to talk to him...

She hesitated, biting her lip and considering this strange notion of—

Ilse's phone suddenly began to ring. A dumb phone. She didn't trust smart phones. She brushed her hair uncomfortably past her ear, feeling a note of anxiety that often accompanied the nagging of any technology.

As she glanced at the number, though, she realized the very devil she'd been thinking of was trying to contact her.

Strange. She had tried to call him a couple of times over the last few days. Occasionally he had answered, but only for a short amount of time. He was embarrassed. She could tell. And she didn't want to stress things. But she also didn't want him to throw his life away. So she'd been insistent, and now, he was calling her.

She picked up the phone, feeling a note of apprehension.

"Tom?" She said, trying to keep her voice cheerful.

She wasn't sure the proper emotion to communicate to someone who'd nearly murdered a man. Not that Ilse thought this made her any better. How many times had she thought about killing her own father? She shivered at the consideration. One of those small, dark thoughts that was never going to see the light of day...

"Doc?"

"Yes, it's me. Is everything okay?"

"Fine," Sawyer said.

Ilse hoped one day she could teach Sawyer a few words that involved more than a single syllable. "How can I help you? Do you need me to come over?" Ilse caught herself. She was being too eager. Too insistent. She didn't want to scare Sawyer off.

"Yeah, you better come over right away," he said.

She tensed, feeling a jolt of excitement. Excitement, because he was finally accepting her offer of help. Nothing more. She was excited whenever a client of hers asked for her help. Not that Sawyer was a client. He was a friend. *Just* a friend. Of course.

And though no one could hear her thoughts, Ilse felt a faint prickle across her cheeks.

"I'm at the office," Sawyer said. "We have a case. See you in a few." The laconic agent hung up.

Ilse blinked at the phone, frowning.

No mention of what had happened at that prison. Not that she'd expected it, especially over a phone call. It was strange to pretend like everything was normal. Then again, wasn't it? No one had known what Sawyer intended. Ilse had gotten there to stop him in time. By the sound of things, he wasn't planning another shot anytime soon.

She supposed there was nothing to do except return to the normal stream of life. With a faint sigh, and a smack to the side of her computer, Ilse pushed to her feet. A case would help her focus. Five days until she flew into Germany. A case would give her the distraction she needed to make it that long.

Besides, catching killers was one of the best ways she could *help*. Every time she spoke with a client, every time she spoke with the survivor of violence, like herself, or Sawyer, she was constantly reminded of one thing: killing a snake was far easier than treating poison.

CHAPTER TWO

Sawyer sat in his car in the parking lot, glaring through the windshield. He wasn't trying to throttle his steering wheel; this was just a happy accident.

Emotions.

He snorted.

Men weren't supposed to have those, were they? Anger. That was his only emotion. Or, at least, had been. But that particular sentiment had gotten him nowhere.

It had seen him walking into a federal prison, intent on taking a life.

Two lives. His included.

But Dr. Beck had shown up. He owed her. He knew that much. Now, in the light of day, he realized what he'd been planning was perhaps not the most advisable course of action. But he was still angry. Furious.

His sister was still dead, and the man who'd taken her was still alive.

Ilse had offered to talk with him. He never would do *counseling*. Absolutely not. But talking? Talking wasn't so bad. Especially if he didn't have to do most of it.

He gave another squeeze of the steering wheel, but then shoved out of the door, marching into the headquarters.

The Seattle field office was different now. As he moved under the cameras, through the metal detectors, and past ample security, he felt a tingle along his spine.

It took him a moment to place the sensation.

Fear.

Sawyer was not a fearful man. He scowled, shifting his shoulders.

"Tom?"

He froze, glancing back towards one of the officers by the door. The cop was adjusting his holster. He waved, pointing towards the conveyor belt by the x-ray machine. "Keys," he said cheerfully.

Sawyer dipped his head, tipping the brim of his baseball cap. He grabbed the keys, and muttered, "Thanks—see ya, Jim."

And then he continued past the checkpoint. No one stopped him.

No one said a thing. And yet, the fear remained.

He had spent so much time on one side of the law that even *glimpsing* the other side was new territory.

He wondered if Rawley knew. Agent Rawley always seemed to be poking in Sawyer's business.

But over the last few days, since his breakdown in that parking lot outside the federal penitentiary...

Nothing.

No internal affairs investigation. No phone calls or visits from the supervising agent. As if it hadn't happened.

Sawyer made his way up the flights of stairs. He stalked through an office section, with multiple cubicles divided by gray screens. At the back of the large conference area, there was a second office. The door was open. He spotted Ilse already standing there. He'd seen her enter the building ahead of him but hadn't wanted to talk at the time.

And now, he was feeling similarly reluctant. He approached the door, hesitantly, wondering if this was a trap after all.

Supervising Agent Rawley was staring through the glass at Sawyer. The man was rigid behind his standing desk. An exercise ball, a bright blue thing, sat next to a floor-to-ceiling window.

Agent Rawley was a bit of a health nut.

A tough nut to crack. But that didn't mean Sawyer hadn't tried. Literally, once. He'd punch to the supervisor.

The man had tried to interfere with Sawyer's business on more than one occasion. At the time, before he'd been suspended, Sawyer hadn't intended to punch his supervisor. But things had piled up. To this day, he couldn't quite remember the exact straw that had broken the camel's back. But one memory stuck out. Rawley prying about Sawyer's sister. Now, as he entered the supervising agent's office, he glanced between Beck and Rawley, frowning.

"Sorry for being late," he said.

Rawley replied, curt, his gaze icy, "Beck says you were sitting in the parking lot."

Ilse winced. "I said I *thought* I spotted you in your car."

Sawyer just shrugged. "Morning meditation."

Supervising Agent Rawley shifted uncomfortably behind his desk. He was wearing a different suit than usual. More blue and pinstripe. Not exactly an agent suit. More like a banker's. He was also shifting behind his standing desk from foot to foot. A nervous energy.

Sawyer felt his nerves returned.

Rawley's hair was combed. The handsome, middle-aged man was the definition of neat and tidy.

But there was an extra effort about it today. Even across the room, as he approached cautiously, Sawyer thought he smelled aftershave.

"You going to the prom?" Sawyer said.

Ilse winced. Rawley just frowned. "I'd appreciate it if you came to our briefings on time in the future."

Sawyer shrugged. Rawley was acting strange. Did he know? Had Dr. Beck told him what happened?

He shot a quick look towards his partner. But no, she wasn't like that.

So he waited, nervously, hiding any glimpse of discomfort.

"Three days ago," Rawley began, slowly, and Sawyer's blood pressure spiked, "I received a very interesting phone call."

Even Dr. Beck was fidgeting now.

Rawley glanced between Sawyer and Ilse. His eyes settled on Tom, narrowing suddenly. "And I'm afraid, Agent Sawyer, I'm going to have to ask you something."

He knew. Of course he knew. Rawley often butted into Sawyer's business. Why *wouldn't* he know? Would Tom end up in prison? He certainly would be fired. He would lose his badge.

He felt like his mind was a caged alley cat, desperately trying to escape its confines with snarls and claws.

But outwardly, his expression was a mask.

He just blinked once, staring at the supervisor.

"Do you think you can be on good behavior?" Rawley said simply.

Sawyer blinked. This wasn't the question he'd been expecting. "I'm always on good behavior," he replied with a straight face. He didn't even glance in Ilse's direction.

"I wish that were true," Rawley said with a long sigh. He folded his hands in front of him on the desk. "The call was from Quantico. As it stands, I'm up for promotion. I don't tell this to you to brag, but to warn." Again he was glaring at Sawyer. "If you cost me this promotion, Tom, by one of your shenanigans, outbursts, illegal arrests, attempts at seducing one of the victims or—"

"That one never happened," Sawyer snapped. "I never seduced a victim."

"Implying the others did," Rawley said with a significant tilt of his eyebrows.

Sawyer glared. He'd walked into that one.

"I'm not trying to make you miserable, Tom. I'm begging you. Don't do anything too much like the sort of thing, er, you *normally* do."

Ilse blinked. "Could you repeat that?"

But both the man ignored her. They were glaring across the desk, their eyes locked. Sawyer was a good ten years younger than Rawley. His hair less gray. His features less cut. Tom's version of a workout was chasing a killer through an alley and tackling him in the mud.

Rawley shook his head. He reached beneath his desk, pulled out a bottle of vitamins and tossed a couple of red gummies in his mouth. He chewed nervously.

He shook his head as he said, "I've been working a long time for this opportunity. I have half a mind to give this case to someone else. But, as we all know, you two have the best closure rate. They're taking a special look at the most recent cases I've supervised. So I'm asking you two, *please*," he added, his voice pleading, "don't do anything to make me regret assigning you both. Dr. Beck, you, I'm trusting, can keep Sawyer in line."

Tom glanced at Ilse. She was nervously brushing her hair in front of her injured ear. She did this whenever she was uncomfortable. Ilse often wore long sleeves and turtlenecks. He noticed this as well about her. She didn't wear makeup. Nor perfume. Occasionally, not that he was paying much attention, he detected the faint scent of lilac deodorant or detergent. Dr. Beck was not someone intent on making an impression. She preferred to stay back, watching. He liked this about her. And then, after a while, done with watching, she would start asking questions.

This part he liked a bit less.

But now, in response to Agent Rawley, Ilse said, carefully, "Sawyer is the senior agent. I'm sure he'll do wonderfully."

Rawley sighed. Sawyer smirked.

The supervising agent waved a hand. "I trust you're right. Now here's what we have; two victims so far. Both of them drugged. Witnesses in the area say they saw a man wheeling them around in wheelchairs. First, they thought the man was some sort of nurse, or helper. Both the victims were young women, but their hair was dyed, and they were dressed in clothing to make them look older."

Sawyer stared at the description. "Just handing us a really run-of-the-mill case now, are you?"

Rawley said, "It's a strange one. I can't choose them. We'll just have to do the best we can."

“So he is drugging them to kill them?” Ilse said.

Rawley turned his attention to her. As he did, his expression seemed less tense somehow. The small vein that throbbed in his temple whenever he was looking at Tom didn’t pulse as badly.

“No, actually. One of the victims was killed by being pushed off the roof of the car park. Still in the wheelchair. She died from the fall.”

Ilse winced. “That’s horrible.”

“The other victim was killed in the same way. She was pushed off an overpass, onto an oncoming truck.”

Sawyer snapped, “Do we have any visuals of the bastard doing it?”

Rawley shook his head. “He avoids cameras. And he wears a hood. A few people noticed the hood. One witness said they greeted the man, but he didn’t reply, and looked nervous... The witness thought the man was hiding something in his pocket. That’s when he got suspicious, and called the police. But by the time they reached the crime scene, the killer was long gone, and the victim was dead.”

“Do we know what substance is being used?” Sawyer asked.

“The coroner is finishing up a toxicology report. It should be available by the end of the day. Also, both victims were killed near the town of Leavenworth. It’s only a couple of hours from here. You know where it is?”

Ilse flinched at the name of the town. Rawley didn’t seem to notice, but Sawyer shot her an askance glance.

Rawley, continued, “Like I said, do your best on this one, and don’t attract any unwanted attention. We have to do this by the book. Is that clear?”

Sawyer muttered, “Break every rule, and beat the witnesses for information. Got it.” He turned, already moving through the door. Ilse sighed behind him. Rawley didn’t even try to call after.

Though, as Sawyer pushed through the door, he did hear the supervising agent mutter to Dr. Beck, “Keep an eye on him. He’s been acting more *Sawyer-like* recently.”

To her credit, Ilse didn’t say anything at all. She followed after, hurrying to catch up in the hall.

CHAPTER THREE

Ilse stood at the edge of the overpass, peering towards the traffic below. A red sedan zipped by, a blur of color. A truck followed close behind, tailgating, and occasionally leaning on its horn. More traffic swept through in the never ending procession of automobiles.

"We were called right after it happened," a voice was saying behind her. "A real mess. I'll be honest, a few of us didn't take it well. We had to shut down the highway. It was a damn nightmare."

She turned back, watching as an older police officer dragged his fingers over his face, and shook his head in exhaustion. Sawyer stood by him, frowning and studying the lines in the older officer's face.

"According to my report, you were the first responder."

The cop nodded at Tom. "I took the witness statements. A couple of motorists pulled over but most commuters just went on their way."

Tom glanced down at his phone, likely reviewing some of the crime scene photos. En route, Ilse had also gone over the pictures. They hadn't been pretty. The coroner was still working on a toxicology report for this first victim. The second crime scene, in the shopping mall, at the top of the parking lot, was on the other side of Leavenworth.

But Ilse had insisted they come to the first crime scene to start, and Sawyer hadn't resisted the suggestion. Ilse, of course, hadn't been completely honest about why she had wanted to start here.

She was familiar with the town of Leavenworth. Familiar with most of the small cities and towns throughout the Pacific Northwest.

Seattle, according to some, was the serial killer capital of the world.

And so, in her line of work, Ilse had familiarized herself with any of the communities touched by the strange epidemic of violence. And Leavenworth, known for its affluence, was known for something else.

Bavarian architecture. It was intentionally styled after a small, quaint, German town. Just like the one she'd grown up near.

Walking through Leavenworth, when she had first visited years ago, had brought back memories she preferred kept dormant.

She mumbled her memory trick, beneath her breath, reciting details of a serial killer who had been active in the region. He'd killed sixteen victims.

She spoke quietly enough so the two men couldn't hear.

"Best we can tell," the officer was saying, pointing to the side, "she was shoved from there. She hit there," he said, subsequently moving the indicating digit.

Sawyer said, "And what did the motorists say?"

The cop glanced at Sawyer's phone. He shifted uncomfortably, looping his thumbs through his belt. A flashlight brushed against his knuckles. "Shouldn't that be in your report?"

"I want to hear it from you."

The cop sighed. "They didn't see much. They were moving fast. As I'm sure you can see. But a couple of them seemed to think they saw someone wheeling the woman along. They didn't think anything of it. At least not at first."

"And did they say what the man looked like?"

The officer shook his head. "They all agreed on that point. He was wearing a hood. To them, it just looked like a nurse wheeling an old woman."

"She was in her thirties, yes?" Ilse interjected, glancing over.

The officer nodded gravely. "Looks like our sicko dressed her up in a sweater and shawl. Dyed her hair. And then he took her for a stroll."

"And was she protesting, trying to run?"

The cop said, "The witnesses didn't see any of that."

"Rawley said they were probably drugged," Sawyer replied. "Maybe they were just being threatened."

Ilse and the officer both shrugged.

Ilse glanced back to the report on the victim. She said, "What do we know about Ms. Perkins?"

"I spoke to her sister earlier today, actually. Tragic conversation." The cop swallowed, running a hand through his silver hair and glancing towards where he had parked under the overpass, next to the stairs.

"What did she say? Any enemies?"

A shake of his head. "I'll send you a voice recording of the interview. You can go through it yourself. I'll include her number, in case you want to make a call. But I don't think she knows much. She said no one would want to hurt her sister. She said Tiffany was lively, rambunctious, friendly, gregarious with everyone she met. Kind. Generous. Not the sort of person you'd expect to make enemies. This creep went after her for some other reason."

"She worked at a hair salon," Sawyer said, raising an eyebrow and glancing towards Ilse.

Ilse nodded, she'd also seen that in the report. "Pricey place," Ilse said quietly. "She would've had high end clients. You don't think this was a money thing, do you?"

The cop interjected here. "We found jewelry on the body. Money in her wallet. This wasn't a robbery."

He trailed off, and the three of them, standing on the concrete structure, listened to the faint swish of motorists below.

Ilse wasn't sure what to do. Part of her wanted to speak to the victim's sister herself—not in order to solve the case, but because she hated the idea of anyone going through something like this alone. Especially without someone to speak to. Her eyes moved to Sawyer, but quickly retreated again. Her fingers grazed the concrete structure at her side. A couple of loose stones flicked free, falling onto the shoulder of the road below.

Ilse frowned. What sort of killer wheeled women off structures to kill them? He had drugged them or at least threatened them. He was getting off on their fear.

This was clear. He liked their *fear.*

"We should go speak with the coroner," Ilse said quietly. "I want to know what he's giving them."

"If *anything*," Sawyer replied. "It's not confirmed they were drugged yet."

Ilse thought Sawyer was just contradicting the theory because Rawley had presented it. By the sound of things, some form of drugging was most likely. Women didn't just let men dye their hair, dress them in old woman's clothing and wheel them around public spaces without trying to scream for help.

No, the killer wouldn't have brought them out in public if he hadn't known he was in complete control. Now, it was up to them to decide exactly what type of control they were dealing with.

The coroner would have to help. The best way Ilse could think of narrowing down a killer, was to find if they had access to a heavily controlled substance. That would do half their leg work for them.

She was already moving, wanting to leave the overpass behind her. The image in her mind of what had transpired there two days before was enough to turn her stomach.

Her feet slapped against the concrete as she picked up the pace, marching back towards where they had parked. If the coroner didn't have answers, then Ilse feared the killer would take another before they could do anything about it.

CHAPTER FOUR

Ilse shot a glance towards where Agent Sawyer lingered in the shadows of the coroner's office. He'd taken up position by a row of sinks beneath a small flickering light that kept turning on and off. He leaned back against the metal basins, his arms crossed.

Ilse returned her attention to the coroner. A younger man, good-looking, with a strong jaw line, and the hands of a football player.

Ilse found herself glancing towards those hands more than once. She thought Sawyer frowned when he caught the look.

She cleared her throat, and said, "Could you say that last part again?"

Dr. Jordan nodded once. He stood with his arms crossed, a clipboard resting on a gurney at his side. The coroner was about a foot taller than Ilse. Taller than Sawyer too. She couldn't help but notice that Tom wasn't slouching like usual.

"I'm afraid it's not good news," Dr. Jordan said, his tone grim. "The killer is using a hybrid substance. It's a watered-down version of the sort of anesthesia they use in most operating rooms."

Ilse winced. "Wouldn't that stuff be heavily controlled?"

"It would be, but it's also relatively common across the states. It's used overseas as well. The thing is, he's doing something to alter it."

"Alter it how?" Sawyer called from his position by the sinks.

Ilse tugged at her sweater sleeves, shivering a bit in the cold room.

Dr. Jordan lifted his clipboard from the gurney, double checking it. "I was worried when I was reading up on the substance. I'm afraid the killer is able to incapacitate his victims. They can't move or speak but they can hear and feel everything"

Those words lingered in the room, even more frigid than the temperature.

"So he's some sort of sadist," Sawyer ventured.

Ilse couldn't help but agree.

"That's not my area," Dr. Jordan said. "Though I'm guessing it wouldn't take behavioral analyst to tell you that." He flashed a smile towards Ilse, and met her eyes for a moment.

Ilse shifted uncomfortably. The attention of an attractive man was never a bad thing. But she'd never dated anyone in her life. She'd had interest at times, as some people thought of her as naturally pretty. But on the other hand, she hadn't thought anyone could handle her background. Damaged goods. That's how she had always thought of herself.

She knew it wasn't the most healthy approach, given her own field, but sometimes, psychiatrists and counselors went into the field for themselves just as much as their clients.

Ilse knew she was a work in progress.

"Is it true the killer dyed their hair?" Sawyer said, glancing towards the wall-to-wall cooling compartments on the other side of the room.

Dr. Jordan didn't even look towards Sawyer. He was still smiling at Ilse. He did say, however, "Hair dye. Yes. Both of them. It looks like the killer also cut Ms. Perkins' hair. He made it shorter, and brushed her bangs in front of her face. I'm guessing he did this so no one could tell she was young. I found traces of hastily cut hair inside her shirt collar."

Ilse shifted, refusing to look Dr. Jordan in the eye. She glanced toward Sawyer and said, "Wasn't that what the cop was saying about the first victim? That she worked at a hair salon?"

Sawyer nodded. "Maybe the killer has some sort of obsession with hair. It would be worth checking out."

Dr. Jordan said, "I have a couple more things that I found interesting. I noticed one of the women was left-handed. You think that's relevant?"

Sawyer shook his head. "You can text the rest. We're heading out." Tom brushed past Ilse, gesturing towards the door.

She gave an uncomfortable glance towards Dr. Jordan, flashed an uneasy smile, then, brushing at her hair, hastened after her partner.

As she caught up with Tom in the hall, she said, "So you think we should check out the hairdressers?"

Sawyer shrugged. "As good a place to start as any. If the killer had experience cutting hair, maybe he was an employee there. Maybe this started as some sort of beauty salon feud."

Personally, Ilse had never set foot in a beauty salon. She had her hair cut by one of her clients.

"A beauty salon feud? That's a thing?"

Sawyer gave a somber shake of his head. "You don't know the half of it, doc. Those places can be vicious. You better watch your back."

It took her a moment to realize he was joking. She frowned as he led the way out of the small, cramped building, up the stairs, and into the parking lot.

CHAPTER FIVE

He leaned back in the green lawn chair. He'd brought it himself to blend in with the rest of them. Though this was more difficult than he'd first anticipated.

He smiled along with the parents, clapping his hands when they did and looking sufficiently flustered at the call of a referee when the faces around him turned sour.

A challenging thing to blend in. Especially amidst all the noise.

He winced as a new wave of cheering arose from the parents. His eyes were fixed on the teenage girls playing soccer.

A varsity game. Seniors in high school sprinting up and down the grass, as if they owned the place.

He could feel his temper threatening to spill over already.

But of course, he couldn't shout. He couldn't yell at the referee. He couldn't make his case to a parent sitting next to him.

No, those options had been taken from him. And so he sat in silence and watched in fury.

He felt someone nudge his arm. He glanced up, sharply. His hand inside his pocket closed over the knife.

"Orange slice?" said a smiling-faced older woman with silver curls. "They had extra. We wondered if the parents would want any."

He met her gaze, and gave a quick, curt shake of his head.

She smiled at him. "No problem. More for the rest of us." She gave a little chuckle, which he was certain she meant to be disarming. Mostly it was irritating.

"Which one is yours?" The woman said, lowering her tray of citrus fruit, and peering at the field.

He didn't reply right away. Instead he watched, still blending in with the parents, pretending to belong. But of course, he wasn't here to root for the sport. He was here for a different type of game. A far more enjoyable type.

And now his gaze was on the star athlete. One of the goal scorers from earlier. A trim, strong looking thing. She had bronze skin, and smiling eyes.

But the thing he noticed most about her was her absolute inability to keep herself in line.

There she went again. Strutting up and down the field as if she were the queen of the world. She scored another goal. Her fists were pumping, her face red with excitement. Other girls crowded around her; parents cheered.

A loud, self-indulgent spectacle. They always were, weren't they?

That was why he'd come after all.

His eyes narrowed as he watched the star player run circles around the corner flag, her arms spread like an airplane.

So full of life, full of excitement and energy. It disgusted him.

"Which one is yours again?" The voice at his side asked a bit more insistently.

He looked at her. He frowned. And then he pointed towards the girl circling the corner flag.

The old woman's eyes narrowed. She set the orange slices on a small cooler filled with water bottles.

She cleared her throat. "That's the principal's daughter. How do you know her?"

The woman's voice wasn't nearly so friendly anymore.

The man just stared, and then, without a response, pushed to his feet. He folded the chair, and, ignoring the protests of the old lady, began to walk away.

"Hang on," the lady was shouting after him. "Don, don't let that man leave. He's a pervert."

But he broke into a jog, running away now.

A few of the parents glanced in his direction. But they were too distracted by the cheering from the recent goal to overhear much.

He kept his chair under his arm, jogging, heading to the parking lot. When he looked back, no one was following.

He slowed, dropping the chair in one of the dumpsters.

He already knew who was going to be next. He would show her how to properly celebrate a success. He had all sorts of interesting ideas in mind.

He reached into his pocket, fiddling with the knife. He adjusted the hood, and raised it, lifting it from his shoulders, and hiding his features.

He would wait until after practice. He'd already found the perfect time to strike. The star player liked to meet up with her boyfriend after the games. And he knew where they went, and what they did.

Young love. It could get someone killed.

CHAPTER SIX

Ilse was impressed by the sheer size of *Carlisle's* Beauty Salon. Plus, the upscale hairdresser's came complete with live entertainment. A faint, crooning voice drifted through the parlor, accompanying the light blues music humming from the speakers hidden throughout the salon.

As Ilse waited by the counter at the front of the shop, she glanced back towards where some women were getting their nails done—others had their heads tilted back, beneath streams of water, while attendants lathered multicolored suds into their hair.

Ilse glanced around, watching, most closely, the employees of *Carlisle's*.

According to the woman at the counter, the namesake of the store had passed years ago, but her daughter now ran the place.

Ilse detected the faint click of heels against polished tile as a young woman, with two crucifix earrings, strutted towards them. Ironically, given her place of employment, her head was shaved.

As she reached the counter, peering between the two agents, she paused long enough to pull a small, grape lollipop from a jar behind the cash register. She removed the wrapper slowly, perfectly manicured fingernails helping in this endeavor. She deposited the wrapper out of sight behind the register and began to lick the grape candy.

Only then did she glance up at them and, in a slow, sultry voice, which Ilse decided was likely practiced to match with the crooning blue's musician, she said, "Welcome to *Carlisle's*. I'm told you two are federal agents."

The receptionist behind the counter shifted next to the phone, tapping her fingers nervously against a glass display case full of high-end shampoos.

"You may go, Candy," said the woman with the lollipop.

The young receptionist named Candy, next to a bowl of candy, nodded gratefully and hurried away, moving back through the beautician section of the salon.

"We appreciate your time," Ilse said with a nod. "We just had a few questions for you. "

"Yes, about Tiffany?"

It took a second for Ilse to recognize the name of their first victim. But then she nodded. "Yes, I'm afraid you must've seen in the news."

Ms. Carlilse licked at the lollipop again, her long nails clacking against the keyboard on the hidden computer behind the register. "A tragedy," she drawled. "I really liked Tiffany. Everyone did."

"That's what we keep hearing," Ilse said with a sigh. "Can you think of anyone who didn't like Ms. Perkins?" Again, her eyes darted to the employees all wearing the black and red uniforms of the beauty salon. These were sleek, trim women. All of them younger than thirty; all of them beautiful in their own right. None of them stood out as suspicious.

But Ilse didn't want to lead with her suspicion. She worried it would make the owner of the salon clam up. Sawyer, on the other hand, who seemed, somehow, to have more experience with such places, came out and blurted, "We think one of your employees may have killed her. Thoughts?"

Carlisle's eyes widened; long, paste on eyelashes fluttered. She placed her fingers to her lips, as if holding back a squeak of horror. "Tell me it isn't so," she declared. The blues musician continued to croon in the lobby.

Ilse winced, shooting a frown toward Sawyer but he just watched the owner of the salon. And then, she started talking.

One moment, she had been playing coy and quiet, sucking on her lollipop. The next, she launched into such an inundation of words, that Ilse almost closed her eyes just to keep up.

"Well of course, there was that issue with Bernie last week."

"Who is Bernie?" Ilse said.

But Carlisle was already answering. "One of my newer hires. She has that cute little poodle of hers. Pink nails. Strange choice, but if you ask me, that's the sort of bold thinking we need around here."

"Wait, the dog had pink nails or the lady?"

"Bernie, dear, try to keep up. Anyway, she and Tiffany had an argument over which of them, one of our newer customers, a Mr. Colbert, was making eyes at earlier. It got downright catty."

"And did this new hire of yours issue any threats?" Ilse said, hesitantly.

"No, no, dear. Nothing like that. Bernie is the absolute sweetest thing. Just like her poodle. And those pink nails of hers. Our patented, candy flavored polish. Would you like to try some?"

She was pointing towards the glass cabinet behind the counter.

Ilse thought she was getting whiplash from the conversation. She tried to keep her tone light as she said, "I don't think we need to bring up Bernie and Tiffany's poodle argument if there were no threats."

"We'll take her information," Sawyer said. He frowned at Ilse, and she shifted uncomfortably. He was right, of course. They couldn't turn down any leads. But she was out of her depth, supremely uncomfortable, and wanting desperately to be someplace else. Places like this made her feel like a fish climbing a tree.

"Anyone else, Carlisle?" Sawyer said, conversationally.

The woman glanced at him. She shrugged one shoulder, and somehow it took three motions, in a dramatic sort of role. "None that I can think of. I would tell you, of course. I'd tell you all sorts of things." She wiggled her eyebrows. Actually *wiggled* them.

Now, Ilse was beginning to wonder if this was how Sawyer had felt in Dr. Jordan's office. She wondered if she ought to just step outside and leave the two of them to speak in private.

Sawyer shook his head. "I appreciate your time. What can you tell us about Tiffany on the job?

"Prompt. Professional. She liked talking, a lot. And coming from me, trust me, that's something."

"Oh, I trust you," Ilse said.

Carlisle beamed at her.

"In fact, sometimes, she spoke a bit more than maybe she should. She once mentioned my marital difficulties with the girls. I told her that in confidence. But I didn't hold it against her. We all have slips of the tongue sometimes. If you know what I mean." Again, she was looking right at Sawyer.

Ilse bit her lip.

"What do you mean *slips of the tongue*?" Tom said, frowning. "Besides the innuendo, I mean. Did Tiffany say something she shouldn't have?"

"Oh nothing specific, dear. Just like what I was telling you. She would occasionally drop hints and secrets that were best left unsaid. Private matters. But who doesn't like a little bit of gossip, hmm-am I right?" Carlisle paused, but then frowned. "Though, again, it can sometimes go too far. I had to fire an employee over something she told me. I really liked Devon. I was sad to see him leave."

Bingo, Ilse thought to herself. Out loud, she said, "Ms. Perkins got someone fired?"

Carlisle bobbed her head, savoring her lollipop for a second, but the lowering it, tossing it in the trash, and saying, "I should be going, I have some books to balance. But, yes. Devon Gibson. One of the older gentleman who worked here. He would sing; as you see we've had to replace him."

"What did she tell you that got him fired?"

"I'm afraid she mentioned that Devon propositioned her. No, not like that. Nothing sordid. He was selling mushrooms. Hallucinogenics. I'm sure you know more about that than I do." She said this part very quickly. A bit *too* quickly. But Ilse was determined not to be sidetracked. "He was a drug dealer?"

"A high end proprietor of hallucinogenic materials," Carlisle said, correcting Ilse. "It wasn't that I'm judgmental of people's lifestyle choices. More that," she hesitated, then trailed off. She tried again, "let's just say I didn't like the business competition on the premises. We're trying to upsell hair product, nail polish. Not blue lagoons."

"I'm taking it that's a type of mushroom?"

Carlisle tapped a manicured nails against her nose. "His own creation."

"You sure seem to know a lot about what he was selling," Ilse said.

Sawyer cut in. "Thanks for your time, Carlisle. Have a good day. You don't happen to have an address for this Devon fellow do you?"

Carlisle had frowned towards Ilse, but then smiled at Sawyer; her lips were very red. "I suppose if you asked nicely I could look for one. Give me a moment. I'll send Candy back with it. Ta-ta." And then, with a dramatic flourish, she began sashaying back through the beauty parlor, towards an office in the rear.

Sawyer watched her leave, and Ilse felt his eyes lingered just a bit longer than absolutely necessary.

She cleared her throat. "She was clearly using mushrooms," Ilse said.

Sawyer shot her a look. "We're not here for drugs. Here for a killer. If this Devon guy was angry enough, and high on his own supply, there's a chance he went after Tiffany for getting him fired. Also, if he knows how to procure that sort of thing, who knows if he can get his hands on anesthesia."

Ilse blinked. "Huh. Not a bad thought."

"I have my moments. Here, hang on, I think that's our address coming towards us."

The receptionist was hurrying back, a small note card clutched in her fingers. It may have been Ilse's imagination, but from here, it looks like someone had pressed a lipstick kiss against the folded paper. Candy handed the note directly to Tom.

CHAPTER SEVEN

Ilse could no longer avoid the town of Leavenworth. Devon Gibson lived smack dab in the center of one of the upscale, cul-de-sac subdivisions. The backyard faced mountains, and she heard the bubbling jacuzzi as they pulled into the driveway.

The town itself, in the rearview mirror, exactly reflected some of her own memories from her childhood.

Bavarian architecture, small, quaint. There was something of a Christmas feel even though they were in the middle of July.

Ilse shifted uncomfortably in the front seat. She didn't like thinking of her past. She could remember many times, heading into town with her father, where he would stop at a small antique store to buy porcelain dolls. He'd been something of a collector.

Ilse could remember sitting in the back of the truck, staring out the window as a little girl. He never let her leave. Not unless she begged and had been on extra good behavior, which just meant her father wasn't in a foul mood.

Which rarely happened

Now, as she had anticipated, the journey through the German-inspired town made her stomach twist. Memories, which she hated, kept trying to surface.

As Sawyer pushed out of the vehicle, she remained seated, breathing slowly in and out.

She thought she heard the sound of a sliding screen door from the direction of the backyard. And then silence. Sawyer circled the car, glancing through the tinted window at her. "You okay, doc?"

She looked up at him, let out a faint puff of air, then rolled up the window, and pushed out herself. "Fine," she said.

Sawyer watched her. "I think I know what this is about."

Ilse hesitated, but let him continue.

"Look, I know we haven't had a drawn out conversation about my actions the other—"

"No. No, sorry, I don't mean to interrupt you but that's not what I'm thinking about."

Sawyer hesitated. "It's not? You okay?"

She nodded as convincingly as she could, then let out a faint, shaking breath. She couldn't help but think of the flight she had booked for Germany. But now, they had to focus on the case. Sawyer, especially, had to be on his best behavior as Agent Rawley was clearly keeping a close eye on him. Ilse had decided the best way to avoid Rawley looking *too* closely, especially after the events the previous week, was to solve the case with as little fuss as possible.

She inhaled, held her breath, counted to seven, and then released it with a long sigh.

It was afternoon. The male blues singer's house was larger than most the ones on the block. The car, in the driveway, was sleek, and painted red. Sawyer stopped to admire it. Ilse had no clue what to call it.

Part of Ilse wanted to check any reports from the BKA agent keeping her appraised of her father's movements. But she decided now wasn't the time. Besides, she didn't get email notifications on her dumb phone, and she didn't want to borrow Sawyer's and let him in on what was transpiring in Germany.

Part of her wondered if this was fair. He had told her what he was dealing with. And yet she refused to return the favor.

She sighed, following after her partner as he moved up the long driveway, strolling between ornate statues and small flowerbeds that had yet to be filled with anything green or growing.

They reached a large front door. Half the frame was glass, while the other was concrete. It was a very strange structure. Ilse guessed it was meant to be artistic. To her, it was more like a migraine.

Ilse couldn't quite tell where one ornate loop began and another ended. A kaleidescope of colors in the form of swooping and swirling patterns ornamented both the glass and the concrete doors, meeting in the middle in a rainbow explosion.

Sawyer rang the doorbell a second time. This time, the insistent sound was met with a patter of footsteps.

"You're early!" a voice called from within the house. Ilse and Sawyer waited patiently, and watched as the door slowly opened. A face peeked out between concrete and glass. The man had a weak chin and he wore large glasses. The hand bracing the door was adorned with an expensive looking watch. All the gears and mechanisms were visible, moving through the glass face. A skeleton watch, if Ilse remembered her terms properly. Her old mentor, Dr. Mitchell *adored* skeleton watches. He considered himself an amateur horologist. She missed Dr. Mitchell, and made a mental note to set up dinner plans as soon as she could.

Her attention returned to the man in the door.

Mr. Gibson blinked at them, glanced past, and then scowled. “You’re not my client.”

“What sort of clients were you expecting, Devon?” Sawyer asked, cheerfully.

It was Ilse’s experience that Tom become most cheerful when criminals were about to have a bad day.

“I—what,” he went quiet, and then tried again. “I don’t know you. Goodbye.”

He tried to shut the door, but Sawyer caught it with his foot.

Ilse winced. She glanced over her shoulder, wondering if anyone was watching. She supposed they were now veering dangerously close to the sort of territory that Rawley had warned them about.

Sawyer, true to form, didn’t seem to care in the least.

“Mr. Gibson,” he said, conversationally, as if his foot wasn’t currently wedged in the man’s front door. “I was wondering if you knew anything about Tiffany Perkins’ recent death.”

The man in the door glared, his eyes flashing behind his glasses. “Who the hell do you think you are?”

Ilse and Sawyer spoke at the same time. “FBI.”

Now, the man just gaped. Ilse watched as the blood left his face.

She didn’t blame him for not recognizing them at first. Sawyer liked to wear jeans, flannel and a baseball cap. She preferred sweaters, and loosefitting slacks. They didn’t exactly scream professional federal agent. But as Rawley had said, their closure rate was hard to beat.

Not that Ilse tracked the sort of thing but Sawyer did, and he often reminded her

“Damn,” said Mr. Gibson with a quick swallow. “Yeah, yeah I think I heard something about that. Awful. Really sad.”

“We heard you had reason to resent Ms. Perkins.”

“Resent her? No. No, no—what? No. She was harmless.”

“She got you fired, didn’t she?” Ilse interjected.

The man’s eyes moved down the door, landing on where Sawyer’s foot was still blocking it. He swallowed, tried to push at the door a bit harder with his small shoulder, but then gave up. Realizing now, they weren’t going to leave on their own, the man’s expression turned once more.

His face prickled with red, and Ilse watched as his temper suddenly burst.

"I don't know what the hell you think you're doing here. But you're not welcome. And I don't see a warrant. So get the hell out of my house. Move your foot. This is private property."

Ilse flinched, remembering Rawley's warnings. She reached out to tug at Sawyer's arm. But he ignored her. Instead, he left his foot exactly where it was.

"How about you come out here, and we can talk like adults. I don't want to have to come in there for you. I'm supposed to be on good behavior today."

Ilse grimaced at this last comment.

The man in the door was blinking between them. His face had turned red again. "What is this? Some sort of joke? Get out of my house!"

His voice was rising in volume. Ilse was worried now one of his rich neighbors was going to start paying attention. Places like this always had cameras. The last thing she needed was for someone at the prison, where Sawyer had snuck into, to recognize him under a different name on some *gotcha* news channel. The less attention they drew to themselves the better.

Sawyer tried to push the door open.

"Tom," she whispered in exasperation.

But Sawyer was predictable in these things. He wasn't the sort to consider his career first and foremost. He had once punched his supervisor, after all.

"Look, tough guy," Sawyer said, his voice turning to a growl. "Come out here. Or I'm going to drag you out."

The man hesitated a moment, but then, with a squeak, and a sudden lurch, summoning some hidden courage, he shoved Sawyer in the chest. He sent the agent stumbling back, and at the same time, he slammed the door.

Ilse heard a faint *click* and then the sound of scampering footsteps.

Sawyer was already moving, circling the house, sprinting through a flower bed. "Check the back!" he shouted.

Ilse sighed. She couldn't have imagined a worse way for that exchange to have gone.

She waited, watching a silhouette dart one way then the next, visible through the glass portion of the door. She stood exactly where she was, and the man, who seemed to want to leave through the front door, kept cursing on the other side.

"I'm very sorry, Mr. Gibson. But we need to speak with you!" Ilse called, wondering if maybe she could defuse the tension.

She heard another squeak from the man, and the sound of a rapid footfalls. A few seconds later she heard the sound of the sliding window.

Sawyer was shouting something, but Ilse could no longer make out his words. She moved towards the side of the house.

And watched as a panicked, small man tried to climb out a first-floor window. It took him a while to do it. It involved a lot of wiggling hips, huffing breaths, and shimmying.

After much effort, with a satisfied grunt, he finally dropped, landing in the garden on the side of his house.

He turned to find himself face to face with the two federal agents

His eyes went wide behind those glasses.

Ilse winced somewhat apologetically as Sawyer leaned in, cuffs at the ready. He said, "Mr. Gibson, you're coming with us."

"I didn't *do* anything!"

"Rule of thumb," Sawyer said, turning the man to cuff him. "If they go out the window, they're guilty."

Ilse decided, as far as personal rules went, this was understandable.

She watched as Sawyer cuffed the man.

Ilse allowed Sawyer to lead the man in cuffs back towards their waiting vehicle.

"Didn't Rawley tell us to use a soft touch?" She whispered, as they pushed the man into the backseat and moved towards the front of the car.

Sawyer glanced at her over the roof of the vehicle. "That *was* my soft touch," he said. "I didn't hit the guy or nothing."

Ilse shook her head in frustration. Sometimes, it almost felt like Sawyer did this stuff on purpose.

The two of them slipped into the vehicle, and Tom, trying his best to hide a grin but failing miserably, started the engine.

Across the street, a couple of neighbors had emerged on the porch. Ilse frowned. One of them looked like they were holding a phone, videoing the exchange. She hunched in her seat, keeping low until they pulled out of the driveway.

CHAPTER EIGHT

"Hang on, hang on, you don't have to take me anywhere. I'll talk."

Sawyer paused, hitting the brakes where he'd been backing out of the driveway. Ilse looked in the rearview mirror. She was met by a panicked, wide-eyed gaze.

"Talk about what?" Sawyer said.

"I didn't *kill* anybody. I know what happened to Tiffany. That sucks. But I had nothing to do with it."

"We'll just take you at your word for it, then. Case solved."

"No, man. I'm not asking you to take me at my word. I'm telling you, I had nothing to do with it."

Ilse said, "Did Tiffany get you fired?"

Devon shifted in the backseat. "I didn't *know* who got me canned. I didn't care, either. I had that gig just to shelter..." he trailed off, and glanced out the window, biting his lip.

Sawyer was frowning. "Mr. Gibson, we're not here about your drug dealing."

Gibson squeaked, looking in the mirror. "Drug? *Drug* dealing?" His voice rose in volume and octave. "My goodness. Who's dealing drugs? That's horrible. Terrible."

"Mr. Gibson?" Sawyer said. "Can you stop?"

The man sagged in his seat, his head drifting towards his cuffed hands. He held his face, moaning and shaking his head. "I didn't do anything. I was nice to her. I would never kill her. Besides, I hear it was some sicko who did it. Pushed her off a bridge or something."

"You know a lot about the case," Ilse said. "Do you know the name Erin Pratt?"

"Who's that?"

Ilse studied his reaction. She turned, no longer using the rearview mirror, but watching where the man sat in the back of the stalled sedan. He was fidgeting uncomfortably. The further they got from his house, the more uncomfortable he looked. Sawyer remained lingering, idling at the base of the driveway.

Ilse said, "That was the second victim."

"Holy crap, there were two? I didn't have anything to do with it.

Who said I did? It was Carlisle, wasn't it? She was angry that I required her to pay my last invoice. This is petty vengeance."

"So how come you tried to crawl out your window?" Sawyer pointed out.

"That wasn't what it looked like."

"Good. Because it looked like a guilty man trying to escape federal officers."

"Man, I'm pretty sure you're supposed to have a warrant before you're allowed in my house."

"I'm pretty sure that people who crawl out windows are hiding something."

Sawyer and Gibson both glared at each other.

Ilse said, "What's in your house, Mr. Gibson?"

She was studying the man, trying to place exactly where he fit in all of this.

She was beginning to wonder if they had made a mistake. He didn't seem like the narcissistic sort. Didn't seem sadistic either. If anything, he looked scared and frightened. Was this the sort of man bold enough to drug his victims and wheel them around in public before pushing them off buildings?

She didn't think so. Then again, she'd been wrong before.

He let out a faint breath, then muttered, "Look, it's probably true. Tiffany got me fired. I didn't know for sure. I was offering her some product, and she didn't like it. But there was no harm. I wasn't in need of the money. Man, look at my house. Look at my car."

"Pretty impressive given a hairdresser's salary."

"I'm not a hairdresser, hotshot," he snapped at Tom. "I sing."

"In the lobby of a hair salon."

"Whatever, man. I didn't kill anybody."

"Well if you keep saying it, it's going to make it true."

Ilse glanced at Sawyer. It was almost like he wanted to rile up their witness. And it was working. His face kept turning from white to red to everything in-between.

And now, he was spluttering again, shaking his head furiously. "What do I have to do to convince you? Look, you know when the murders took place? I could tell you where I was. I've had clients all week."

"What sort of clients?" Ilse said.

He sighed. "The people who live around here, man. They're nice people. Easy to get along with. And they don't bring a piece to a deal."

"Forgive me if I'm not familiar with your vernacular," Ilse said. "By piece, I take it you mean weapon? And by deal, I take it you mean hallucinogenics?"

He went silent again. Sawyer growled. "You have to give us some reason to trust you here, Devon."

"I don't like the way you say my name," the man muttered.

"Take it up with your parents, *Devon*."

"Look, fine, I make a little extra cash on the side. Sue me."

"Quite possibly. After we arrest you."

Another panicked flare of the eyes. "No, come on, don't do that. I didn't kill anyone. I gave some people a slight buzz, and a nice high. I'm providing a public service. My wares keep people from hurting others. It's just harmless fun."

"So you admit you were dealing drugs?" Sawyer said.

Ilse decided perhaps there was a method behind the madness. Devon Gibson was so flustered, he was saying things he would likely later regret. Things he probably wouldn't have said at a police station. But now, close to his own home, in the back of the car, he was struggling to get them to believe him.

"I crawled out the window because I have some samples in the house that probably won't look good on an arrest report."

"What sort of samples?"

"What do you think, man? Urine. Salsa. What's with all the questions."

"Questioning you is my job," Sawyer said. He was sounding bored now.

Ilse knew that tone. Sawyer sounded like this whenever he started to doubt if they had the right suspect. Tom was tough on criminals who killed people. But non-violent offenders often led to him quickly losing interest.

"So you're saying you ran because of the drugs you have in your house?" Ilse said.

He muttered now, shaking his head. "Look, I said a bunch. You have to believe me, I didn't kill anybody."

"Where were you on Saturday night?" Two days ago, the time of the first murder. She waited, studying him.

He clicked his tongue, thinking desperately, and then his eyes widened. "Th-the nice couple across the street. They're filming you right now. I had a appointment with them. If you ask them, tell them I said it was for yoga."

"What if I asked them if they were buying drugs from you?" Sawyer said.

"Man, you want me to get in trouble? These people have money. They'll actually sue me for defamation or some shit."

"They *won't* actually *arrest* you."

Devon sighed. "If you lead with the drugs, they're not going to tell you a thing. But if you tell them we had yoga, they might be honest. I was at their house. Well into the afternoon. We were doing a big deal. They have this country club, on this golf course. They were setting up deals of their own."

Ilse blinked. "They were buying mushrooms from you to sell at their country club?"

"Don't look at me like that. My stuff is way safer than most the sorts of things you hear about it in places like this."

Ilse shook her head. "I can't say I hear about any of it."

"Well, aren't you special. But those two were with me for like five hours. From noon until four."

"That's not five hours," Sawyer said.

"Man, what do I look like, a mathematician?"

Ilse glanced at the glasses, at the thin arms and the nervous disposition. She decided not to answer the question

"Alright; so let's say we ask them about yoga; will it account for all four of those hours?"

He nodded readily, swallowing as he did.

Sawyer slowly shared a look with Ilse. The timeframe he had given covered when the murder was committed. The witnesses on the highway had called it in at about two in the afternoon.

Ilse bit her lip, and Sawyer shook his head. He pointed right at Mr. Gibson. "I'll be right back. If you're lying, I'm going to be pissed."

"Yeah man, cuz you've been a real bucket of smiles so far."

Sawyer hid another smirk, but forced a scowl back in place.

And then he shoved open the door, leaving the car running, and marched across the street, towards the couple filming them on their camera.

CHAPTER NINE

The postcards weren't working. She simply wasn't getting the message. So he had decided to write with letters she couldn't possibly miss.

He strolled up the sidewalk, nodding politely as a young man pushed open the apartment door. He shifted the mailbag over his shoulder, adjusting his blue postman's cap. The man held the door open for him.

Technically, this made the young man an accomplice.

He smirked, rushing past, and moving into the apartment.

As the door slowly swished shut behind him, cutting off the faint breeze from the outside, his eyes scanned the post boxes

He knew everything about Ilse. He'd been researching her extensively for years. Ever since she had made that fateful choice.

It was as if she didn't even remember him. Didn't even think her words had unintended effects.

Words could hurt, after all.

But in his experience, there were better ways to cause pain.

Standing in the lobby, allowing for the moment, he allowed his mind to wander back to those horrible moments after she had given him the news.

He had wanted to kill himself. He had never wanted anything so badly

But of course, he chose another path.

He wanted her to feel the same way she had made him feel.

And so he had taunted her. Sent her messages. She was *supposed* to kill herself just like he'd wanted to do.

But she was stupid or something. He couldn't quite place his finger on it. It was as if she didn't care. Maybe she just didn't remember. Maybe that was it. It was up to him to remind Ilse Beck where she came from. Little Hilda Mueller. Pretending to be something she wasn't.

Which, of course, was what he was now doing. He smirked at the comparison, taking the steps now, moving up towards her apartment. It had all been so easy.

This time, he was going to kill her himself. And he was going to do it slow. Everything was ready. He had all the tools he needed in his fake mailbag.

As he took the stairs, moving into the dingy building, he pulled the small lockpicking set from his pocket.

His skills were a bit rusty but this was the perfect time to practice. Besides, he'd been watching her for weeks. She didn't often come home until late in the evening, especially when she had a case.

He was going to wait, and then, when she returned, he was going to have some fun. H felt certain, she would remember who he was.

In fact, he might even give her a choice. More torture, or she could kill herself. That way, they could both get what they wanted.

CHAPTER TEN

Ilse pushed through the small break room door at the precinct. Sawyer was already sitting at the table by the vending machine, shaking his head, and sipping on a small cup of coffee.

She pointed at the cup. “Out of caffeine pills?”

He grumbled, still shaking his head. “I can’t believe his alibi checked out. What sort of idiots admit to a drug deal?”

“I thought you said you asked them about yoga.”

“I did. But obviously it wasn’t yoga. Did you see the two of them? The furthest they’ve stretched was across the couch to grab the remote.”

Ilse shook her head, sitting at the break room table of the small, Leavenworth police department.

Devon Gibson was still being interviewed by the other officers. But Sawyer didn’t care about the drug charges, and Ilse wasn’t going to undercut his decision. Eventually, by the looks of things, Mr. Gibson was going to walk.

His neighbors had confirmed what he’d told them. He couldn’t be the killer as he’d been occupied at the time of the first murder.

Which led them back to square one.

“I’ve been looking at our second victim’s case file,” Ilse said quickly, leaning across the table to meet Sawyer’s gaze. “She was a door-to-door salesman. Maybe she accidentally rang the wrong doorbell. I was wondering if we could possibly go through the addresses she visited.”

Sawyer shook his head. “Can’t. I tried.”

She frowned. “When?”

“When you were just in the bathroom. Geez doc, you took a while. You okay? You look stressed.”

Ilse wrinkled her nose. She had been standing in front of the sink, breathing in steam from the faucets. Another soothing trick she had learned. She still was not comfortable in the Bavarian style town. And for whatever reason, she still wasn’t willing to talk to Sawyer about it. He wasn't the sort of person to pry... If anything, he didn't talk much at all. But in the past, whenever she'd shared something, he'd been an avid and interested listener. But with Tom... It felt like wanting to peel back a bandage.

She adopted a look of offense. “You often make a habit of commenting on a woman’s restroom breaks?”

Sawyer held up both his hands. “Sorry. Wasn’t trying to offend. But I *did* call them. They don’t track addresses. Technically it’s a legal. I bet you they do, but they’re not going to admit it to us.”

“Do you think Rudiger might be able to have access to –”

“No. I’m not calling him. Not after last time. He keeps trying to set me up with...” Sawyer trailed off and took a sip from his coffee cup through pursed lips.

“With who?”

Sawyer glanced at the rising steam. “It won’t matter anyway. I don’t think we’re looking for an address. We should look for a connection between them.”

“The victims?”

“That’s right. One of them was a salon worker. In her twenties. The other a door-to-door sales woman in her thirties. One of them cute. The other average-looking.”

“Which one was cute?”

“Focus, doc. Look, all I’m saying is, I don’t know if we’re looking at this right. Maybe the victim -type isn’t the point. I was wondering if it’s some sort of medical thing. I checked out their blood type. Different.”

Ilse frowned. “Different hair color. Different eye color. Different towns. Different religions.”

“How do you figure the religion thing?”

“I looked through the report that the one officer had with Ms. Perkin’s sister.”

Sawyer tapped his nose and pointed at her. “Good thinking. Anything fresh?”

Ilse slouched, resting her chin against the back of her hands, and leaning on the table. “Nothing that stood out.”

Tom tapped his steaming mug. “What if they’re random? What if there is no connection but he’s just picking them out of the crowd?”

“Well,” Ilse said, considering this option. “It’s possible. Definitely possible. It would make our job a lot harder.”

“True.” Sawyer leaned back, crossing his hands behind his head, the bill of his baseball cap tipping up.

“Your phone’s ringing,” Ilse said, detecting the faint buzzing sound from the device face down on the table.

Sawyer waved a hand. "It's Rawley. He called a couple of times already. I'm sending him to voicemail."

"What does he want?"

"Same stuff. He's up for promotion. Wants to put the pressure on. Yadda yadda. His management style is a little more hands-on than HR should allow."

Ilse shook her head. She watched Sawyer, studying his green eyes, the faint stubble along his chin

"I don't know how you do it," she said at last.

"Do what?"

"Live at war with the world. With everyone."

Sawyer nodded. "Is that your professional opinion?"

"It's *an* opinion. Am I wrong?"

"Are we talking about the case now, or about me?"

Ilse shook her head. "It's just I've never seen someone with so much fight in them. It's not an insult. In a way it's impressive. You just don't back down. Sometimes, I wish I was like that."

She thought back to her childhood. Thought back to the number of times she *had* backed down. When she hadn't come through. Her siblings had been hurt because of her failings. The guilt still ate at her.

Sawyer was studying her now with the same intensity she'd been using on him. "What about you?" He said, watching her over the wafting steam from his cup of coffee. "You've got fight. You've also got secrets. I know that much. Lot of plane rides for someone who's just a local counselor."

Ilse sighed. Sawyer knew a bit about her father. A bit about Germany. But not much. She didn't share much of her personal life with anyone. Not even Dr. Mitchell, her old mentor, and her own counselor, knew the full extent of her life experience.

In fact, when she thought about it, no one knew. At least no one who cared about her. Her father knew but that only made her furious.

"I guess both of us are a bit unusual," Ilse said, hoping to bring the discussion to a quick conclusion. She was growing uncomfortable. These were not the sorts of things she liked to talk about.

But Sawyer was like a dog with a bone. He seemed to have latched onto something of interest, and wasn't intent on giving it up.

"I think your tougher than you give yourself credit for. At least that's what I've seen. It wasn't for you," he said, slowly, "I wouldn't be sitting here."

Ilse glanced towards the break room door. No one was in the hall. They were alone. She wasn't sure what to say to this.

If there was ever a chance to speak more about what had occurred back in that prison, Sawyer had just given her the opportunity.

But a part of her wasn't sure she wanted to talk about it. Not now. Not yet. She had a plane ride in five days to deal with her father in Germany. She'd agreed to go and keep tabs on him. To help the BKA put him back behind bars.

She wasn't sure if Sawyer would understand any of it. How could he?

People who didn't experience trauma themselves growing up often lived their lives thinking somehow they were whole and others were harmed.

They liked to think of the mountains they climbed as accomplishments. But the pits and chasms that others clambered out of, with painstaking, backbreaking work, only to arrive at the foot of the mountain they had scaled, was nothing more than laziness.

Ilse had never felt much camaraderie towards people who'd lived without pain.

But Sawyer wasn't like that, was he?

He knew pain. His sister's death haunted him

"We should get coffee," Sawyer said.

She blinked as if he'd slap her. She stared. "Excuse me?"

"Not this," Sawyer said, shaking the cup in front of him. "Like a date," he said, without looking at her now. He was brushing it off as casual, nonchalant. But she noticed the way his fingers were tapping the table. It was coming out of the blue. At least, that's what it felt like. But now, she spotted the way he was glancing at her when he didn't think she was looking for.

"A date?"

"Yeah. A date. You've been on those before, right?"

He was trying to be funny. But she said, "No. I haven't"

He leaned forward, tilting his cap. "Wait, really?"

She shook her head once. "I'm afraid not."

"You're like thirty, aren't you?"

She didn't correct him. There was no sense adding a couple of years. "I'm aware, but I've never dated anyone. I'm sorry if that disappoints you."

Tom considered this, but then he just grinned. "It doesn't bother me. Shoot, if anything it's a plus. I'm horribly unromantic. I can use all my old tricks. Flowers, chocolates."

"I read books and watched TV, Tom. I'm aware of the theory behind it."

Sawyer crossed his arms over his thin chest. "Is that a yes?"

Ilse let out a faint sigh. She wasn't sure what to say. She had always denied herself this particular form of connection. She had known that it would take a mountain of work to ever navigate a relationship with someone else. Especially given her past. How could she explain her nervous tics? How hard it was to sleep? The screaming at night sometimes? How could she explain her fear of the dark? Her *many* fears...

But as she watched Sawyer, she realized if anyone might understand, it was him. And yet, somehow, this only scared her all the more.

She traced her fingers across the table, biting her lower lip.

"I-I don't want to offend you. But I don't know what to say. I need to think."

Sawyer swallowed. The gesture was quick, though. And he covered with a faint shrug. "I'll take that. Thinking is good. I mean, no rush. No hassle. Just, you said you wanted to talk. I thought maybe that would be a good way to–"

"You're right. It would be. I just-it's not *you*, Tom."

"Right. You really haven't done this before,?"

Again, she could tell he wasn't trying to hurt her. She shook her head. Her hair swishing. She studied her fingernails, if only to have something to look at.

And that's when Ilse's phone began to ring.

Saved by the bell.

She felt a flash of relief and fished the device from her pocket, lifting it. She answered, "Dr. Beck."

It was Rawley. "Dammit, Agent Beck, why the hell is Tom not answering?"

She winced. "Apologies, sir. He was working on the case."

"Jesus Christ, Ilse, the case is why I'm calling. There's another body. You two need to get the hell over there. Christ," he repeated, with even more disgust. "I'm sending the address now. Hurry. And I mean *now.*" He hung up.

Ilse winced, slowly lowering the phone. She looked at Sawyer.

"He sounded mad," Tom said cheerfully.

"He's not happy," Ilse murmured. She was pushing out of her chair, still flustered, but now starting to feel a jolt of anxiety replacing the sense of discomfort. Another body. Another murder. They were still no closer to solving this. She felt as if she was scooping her hand through a bucket of sand, the grains passing between her fingers.

More and more, she was starting to feel as if she didn't quite have a grasp on her own life. As if somehow, things were just outside her control.

Sawyer had sobered at the comment. He was already downing the rest of his coffee, and then he crumpled it, tossing it in the waste bin as he hurried after her, exiting the breakroom. Ilse's phone buzzed with the new address for the newest victim.

CHAPTER ELEVEN

Night had fallen now. Though perhaps it was more accurate to say it collapsed.

And the resounding silence of its tumble was still reverberating around the small school building, facing the soccer field.

Ilse and Sawyer stood on the edge the grass, under the night sky, staring in the direction of the goalpost.

Both of Sawyer's hands were bunched into fists. Ilse had tears in her eyes.

She was reminded of her own sister. Reminded of how things ended.

"I hate him," Sawyer murmured, staring at the goalposts.

Flashing lights of red and blue streaked the sky. The reverberating sirens shook the windows of the school beyond. Cops in the parking lot were holding back gawkers and onlookers. More than one phone, being used to record the scene, had been confiscated.

There was a tension on the air.

Ilse's eyes scanned the figure hanging from one of the goalposts.

Her hair was streaked gray. Her head cocked to one side, her legs and arms limp like lead.

Dead. She was only eighteen. Her whole life ahead of her.

"They found a wheelchair," a cop was saying, standing a few paces away and shifting nervously. The young woman could see the fury in Sawyer's gaze. Spotted the tears on Ilse's face.

Ilse quickly wiped at her cheeks and turned to face the officer.

The cop winced, but waved the clipboard towards the trees beyond the soccer field. "Finding trace evidence that she was in the wheelchair. Looks like he pushed her around, and then use the chair to..." she trailed off, and waved a hand towards the goalposts.

Ilse bit her lip so hard she drew blood. She resisted the urge to spit, and instead swallowed the copper taste.

"Do we know if she was drugged too?" Sawyer murmured.

The officer shook her head. "They're asking the coroner. But there's nothing conclusive yet."

Ilse's eyes moved towards forensics, who were milling by the body.

A couple of them were raising a ladder to help cut the body down from where it dangled.

Behind her, Ilse could hear someone crying. She looked back to see an older woman leaning against a tall man in a suit.

The man, she had been informed, was the principal of the school.

This was his daughter.

Ilse's eyes fixated on the tall man. He stared resolutely, unyielding. His wife leaned against him, sobbing into his chest.

The tall principal look shellshocked. Exhausted. But he didn't even blink as he stared towards where his daughter had been hung.

"From what I gather she was something of a star," the officer at Ilse's side was saying. She shifted uncomfortably in the grass, her foot scraping across a white line painted over the turf.

"I looked her up on the way over," Sawyer said, his voice grim. She scored two goals in the last match. They were celebrating."

"I'm afraid it's worse," whispered the officer. She cleared her throat, though, summoning volume and said, louder, repeating, "I'm afraid it's worse. We found her boyfriend's car."

Ilse said, "Where's her boyfriend?"

"He's in the car. The killer cut his throat."

Ilse felt like she wanted to collapse.

There was something particularly heinous when the young were targeted. She tried to focus, though. It was difficult under the night sky. Exhaustion heavy. Emotions running high. The sound of tears behind them.

Sawyer was similarly bothered by the noise. He shook his head in disgust. "Why are we letting them see this? It's going to haunt them. We should keep them back."

The officer shook her head. "They refused to leave. I didn't think it was right to–"

Sawyer rubbed a hand through his hair. "Christ. Dammit. All right, focus." He was speaking to himself more than anyone else. He slapped his own face, shaking his head. He inhaled slowly, and determinedly looked away from the body dangling from the goalposts. He looked at the officer now. "Make sure they photographed that car. How far away was it?"

"In a small parking spot on the side of a bike path in the forest. Private, secluded." The officer shifted uncomfortably. "We found a condom. It hadn't been used yet. We think they had gone off to have some fun after the game. According to the principal, he didn't know where his daughter went but he knew she often spent time with her boyfriend."

Sawyer nodded. "Don't mention the condom to them." Cop shook her head. Sawyer turned to Ilse, and said, "You're going to have to take the lead, doc. It's going to take something of a gentler hand than I have."

Ilse nodded, and then followed after Tom as they began to move towards the principal and his wife.

Sawyer lingered back as they drew near, allowing Ilse to take the lead. There was nothing less she wanted to do in the world. But this was why the FBI had hired her. This was her field of expertise.

It never got easier. The tears, the pain. It never got easier, and Ilse never wanted it to.

She stood facing the two of them, and cleared her throat softly. "Mr. and Mrs. Sanderson?"

The principal didn't even seem to hear. His eyes were glued on where they were cutting his daughter down from goalposts. His wife looked up, her eyes streaked with tears. She met Ilse's gaze, and then tugged at her husband's arm. "Peter," she whispered. "Peter, dear," she said, her voice shaking.

Finally, the principal of the school looked down. He blinked a couple of times, shaking his head. He had receding hair and glasses perched on his nose. He looked more like a stern librarian than a principal. He also was wearing a tracksuit and smelled faintly of sweat, suggesting he had been working out on a nighttime jog when they'd notified him.

Ilse let out a faint sigh. There was never a good place to start. So she just started. "I'm very sorry. Do you think it might be better if we moved away from the scene?"

Peter didn't say a word. He just stared at her, shellshocked. His wife, sniffing back some tears, and dabbing at her eyes said, "No, that's fine. Are you police?"

"FBI. That's my partner. Again, I'm so, so very sorry. We're doing everything we can," Ilse trailed off. She decided it probably wasn't best to remind these two that if they had caught the killer, their daughter would still be alive. So she redirected. "This is probably a horrible time, but I was wondering if you heard anything from your daughter tonight. Any calls, text messages?"

Mrs. Sanderson shook her head. "We were both at the game. It was only a few hours after that we got the call from the police."

She bit back a sob, and forced her words to remain steady. She continued, her eyes flashing fiercely, “It was such a happy day. Winning that game meant they were going to go to Washington DC for a tournament. Riley was so happy.”

“Can you tell us anything about Riley at the game?” Ilse said, slowly, her tone gentle. “Was there anything unusual? Anyone there that shouldn’t have been?”

The principal’s wife was shaking her head. “Nothing. Not that I can think of. Sometimes, we have people who come by and watch the girls play. I heard there had been some issues with men from the bike path stopping to watch.”

Peter shook his head. “That’s what we get for moving to a city,” he said. Now that he was speaking, his voice was like his posture. Firm, strong. There was no sign of emotion in his tone.

In a way, it reminded her of Sawyer. But in another way, it was the saddest thing she’d ever heard.

“It’s usually harmless,” Peter said. “Some of the students, or a few of the athletes in other programs like to come and watch... harmless...”

“You repeated that,” Ilse said, slowly. “Can I ask why? Harmless in what way?”

She wasn’t sure why she was asking. More of a fishing expedition, really. But she had always known to pay attention to the words people repeated when in her office.

The principal shook his head with a sigh. “Some of the parents came to me a few months ago and wanted to have admissions for the games. They said people were coming who didn’t belong. Strangers with bad intentions for wanting to watch the girls. And in a way, I understood. But a lot of times, the people they were concerned with turned out to be students at the school. It’s not up to me to decide who can watch what for what reason.”

He was speaking somewhat defensively now. Ilse noticed his wife was no longer leaning against him. But instead was looking off into the trees, frowning.

“I take it you didn’t agree with this decision?” Ilse said.

Mrs. Sanderson shook her head. “If you like the sport, that’s one thing. But some of these guys were jeering, catcalling. It was fun for them.”

“And were they there today?” Ilse said.

The principal shook his head. But Mrs. Sanderson replied, “I actually heard from Donna Bristow’s mother, that there was someone at the field wearing a hood. He was watching the girls. When asked about who he was there to see, he pointed at," she held her breath, and let out a faint sigh. "At our daughter." Her voice cracked, and she broke into another round of sobbing.

Ilse wished she had a tissue to offer. Wished she could just reach out and hug the woman. But she decided this would only make things worse.

She said, "Did you get a description of the guy?"

Peter pointed towards the officer they had been speaking with. "She took a statement from Mrs. Bristow. But she doesn't remember anything. She just said the man was pale and weird."

"And does that fit the description of anyone who you were concerned about a few months ago?" Ilse said, glancing towards Mrs. Sanderson.

"I couldn't say. Yes, of course. But it's not much to go on."

Sawyer was moving back in the direction of the officer. Ilse watched him leave for a moment. She supposed he was likely about to get the statement that had been given. She returned her attention to the principal and his wife. "Do you think I could get the names of the spectators causing problems?"

Mrs. Sanderson shook her head. She snapped. "It's *two* names. The same problem every time. He would leave illicit comments on school field trip photos about some of the girls. He's a senior in the school. A troublemaker. The only reason he still here, is because his father would sometimes come with him. Also occasionally defend his son's comments towards the players... It was disgusting to see a grown man stand up for that sort of talk. Besides, the father has money in—"

"Stop," Mr. Sanderson said sharply. He glared at his wife. "That's not the reason."

Ilse frowned. "Sorry, what reason?"

Mrs. Sanderson glared at her husband. She said, "Well? Do *you* want to tell her?"

Ilse glanced politely at the tall man. He let out a long breath, then said, "We had some behavioral issues with Carter—an... an allegation of sexual harassment. But no one ever testified. We crossed all the t's, dotted the i's, but nothing we could do. Plus, he's a good basketball player. He had a scholarship, and we thought it was going to work out."

The principal shook his head, staring towards where his daughter's body was now beneath the tarp, being wheeled towards the parking lot and the waiting ambulance.

"If that's all," the tall man said, curtly, "I have some newsletters to send out, and I don't even know how I'm going to tell Jason."

Mrs. Sanderson broke into another round of sobbing.

"Who is Jason?" Ilse asked.

"Our son," Mrs. Sanderson said softly. "But the name you're looking for is Carter Thompson. He would watch the girls play, and often make comments. He upset more than one of the mothers. If anyone did this," she said, her voice shaking with rage, "it's that little monster. And his father was there, too, half the time. Hell, I think I once heard him shouting things also to girls half his age."

Ilse didn't comment on this last part. She could see the grief, the rage, and the way that the two of them were turning cold on each other. It had not been her intention to divide them. Mr. Sanderson was glaring across the field. Mrs. Sanderson refused to look at her husband now.

Ilse knew it wasn't her place, and yet she couldn't help herself. She cleared her throat, leaned in, and said, "I know it's none of my business. But I actually work in counseling. You're not asking, and you can hate me for saying it, but the people who I see make it out the other side, intact, are the ones who do it together. You're not angry at each other. Not really. At least not over this."

She wasn't sure what she was saying. It certainly wasn't the best phrased comment. And in a way, it felt presumptuous. She didn't know their marriage. Didn't know their situation.

But she knew one thing. If they tried to grieve alone, or if they used this as an excuse to get angry at one another, it wouldn't just cost them their marriage, but also their family.

"Jason is going to need you both," she said with a shrug. She nodded once, and then turned, not wanting to see their reactions and moving back towards Sawyer.

She wasn't sure *why* she'd said it. Even walking away, she felt the urge to cringe. It hadn't been her place. It was none of her business.

And yet she couldn't just sit idly by.

Because it was her fault.

A small voice whispered at her.

If she had done something, and found the killer in time, Riley Sanderson would still be alive. Riley's boyfriend would still be alive.

Four victims now.

Ilse could feel a sour taste in her mouth. As she rejoined Sawyer, he was finishing up his conversation with the officer. He looked at her, and said, "No description."

“Think we should call her ourselves?”

Sawyer nodded. “I have the number. But by the sound of things, the lady was handing out orange slices and didn’t see anything.”

“Orange slices?”

“That’s what she said she was doing,” the officer interjected, nodding. “She said she saw a man she didn’t recognize watching the girls.”

“Well, Mrs. Sanderson says a kid named Carter Thompson is likely to blame.”

Sawyer massaged his temples, letting out a long sigh. “Think it’s possible that our hooded guy is Carter?”

Ilse shook her head. “No clue. There is no saying if Mrs. Bristow knows who that is.”

“She doesn’t,” the officer interjected. Ilse frowned. “You asked about him?

The officer nodded. “Mrs. Sanderson mentioned his name to me, so I thought I should float it by the only witness we had. I didn’t have time to set up a lineup. But given the description she provided, it’s possible she did see Carter Thompson. The man in the hood, according to her, was taller than average, and pale. She said he moved fast. And he didn’t talk much.”

“Taller than average—Carter is a basketball player,” Ilse said slowly. “I know it isn’t much... but...” Ilse shared a look with Sawyer.

Tom shrugged once. “How are you feeling, doc? It’s getting late.”

“Not on your life am I turning in yet. We still have to catch this guy. Tom, I’m serious, I refuse to let him have another. I will *not* speak to another family about this guy’s victims. We’re going to catch him.” Ilse hadn’t meant to speak so fiercely. But Sawyer wasn’t disagreeing. He gave a brief nod, thanked the officer, and then turned towards her, gesturing for her to follow.

“We should probably check out the car by the river, and then I’ll call Mrs. Bristow to confirm what she saw. But then let’s head to a Carter Thompson’s place, and see if we can find anything. What exactly did Mrs. Sanderson accuse him of?”

“Ogling the girls. Rude comments on the field—his dad apparently joined in at least once. Carter was also accused of sexual harassment, but it was dropped.”

Sawyer nodded. “I’m finding it difficult to think, though, that a high school kid could get his hands on anesthesia. Not unless,” he frowned. He fished his phone from his pocket.

"What?"

They moved along the grass, keeping in line with the whites, painted line.

"You mentioned his dad. I'm looking what he does for a living."

Sawyer his phone glowed, illuminating his face as he hastily entered the information of their newest suspect.

Ilse picked up the pace, moving in the direction of the commotion by the bike path where the car and the other body had been found.

Had the killer gotten sloppy? Was it possible he left DNA evidence?

She wasn't counting on it.

She heard a faint hiss, and Sawyer said, "Bingo."

"What is it?"

"Carter Thompson's dad works as a pharmaceutical re."

Ilse frowned. "That might give him access to the anesthesia and the wheelchairs. You don't think his father has something to do with it too, do you?"

"I've heard of weirder. No clue. Let's check out the car, and see if there's anything there—then go speak to the Thompsons."

CHAPTER TWELVE

Ilse sat in the car, her cheek pressed against the cold glass of the passenger-side window, her eyes tracking the many lights flashing by on the side of the highway as Sawyer picked up the speed. She listened to him murmuring on the phone, confirming details with the only witness who had spotted the man at the soccer competition. She could hear the frustration in her partner's voice. They weren't getting anywhere.

At last, Sawyer said, "Thank you, Mrs. Bristow, I appreciate your time. I'm very sorry about everything. Have a good evening." He hung up.

Ilse glanced towards the dashboard. It was nearly ten. Well past *good evening.*

"Any luck?" she asked, glancing at her partner.

Sawyer let out a long sigh. "Nothing. She barely saw the guy. Said she was focused on his hands."

"Why?"

Sawyer muttered, "Because apparently a few months ago they had an incident where someone was flashing obscene gestures at the players. Our guy Carter, she said."

Ilse wrinkled her nose, scowling. "You serious? What sort of perverts do that?"

Sawyer looked at her. "Carter Thompson. He was taken in for disciplinary action."

"So it was him?"

Sawyer shook his head. "Mrs. Bristow wasn't sure. No one else saw him."

Ilse shook her head, frowning. "I heard back from Mrs. Sanderson. Looks like Carter was a friend of Jamie—Riley's boyfriend. Seems like he might've been able to approach the car without spooking them. There's a chance he attacked his friend, then took Riley."

Ilse didn't want to picture the crime scene they'd visited by the bike path. The small, rusted sedan had looked as if it had simply been idling under the trees. But then she'd seen the body. Jamie's neck slit.

No sign of a shattered window, or broken lock. The killer had somehow gotten access to the car without disturbing the two high schoolers.

This fit with the theory that it was someone they had known.

Ilse glanced at the speedometer as Sawyer picked up the pace, racing in the direction of the Thompsons' home. Ilse reviewed the evidence in her mind. It seemed to fit. Especially since Craig Thompson, Carter's father, was in pharmaceuticals. The company he worked for had access to the same sort of anesthesia that would have been used by the killer. According to witnesses, Craig *and* Carter Thompson had caused a disturbance at the soccer games.

What if it was a father-son team?

A faint chill trembled down her spine as she considered the horrible possibility.

***

Sawyer's fist barked against the wooden door, and the first response came in the form of a porch light. After doing some research, Ilse had determined the Thompson parents were currently separated. Carter lived alone with his father.

She heard the sound of voices on the other side of the door. The small, single story home was set against a backdrop of large trees and deep greenery.

The voices continued a moment longer, and then Ilse heard the sound of the chain rattling, then the door opened. A young man stared out at them. He was tall, shirtless, and wearing basketball shorts. Behind him, a young woman was wearing a long shirt that barely covered her legs.

Sawyer shifted uncomfortably.

The young man in the door scowled. "Who are you?"

"Are you Carter Thompson?"

The girl shifted uncomfortably, smoothing the shirt past her legs.

"Who's asking?" The teenager said.

"Agent Sawyer," Tom said, his voice firm, flashing his badge. "We need to speak with you, Carter."

The girl behind him was now looking uncomfortable. "What's this about?" she whispered.

But the lanky athlete shushed her with a quick shake of his head. "I didn't do nothing."

"Could you step onto the porch, please."

"Shit, whatever. Can I grab a shirt?"

"She can grab one for you," Sawyer replied.

Carter Thompson shrugged, and moved onto the porch, yawning as he did, as if he had all the time in the world.

Ilse glanced past him, frowning. "Carter, is your father home?"

"No. He's out."

Sawyer shot Ilse a look. Murmuring, he said, "How close are we looking at the father?" He allowed his voice to carry an inflection that she couldn't quite place. But he waited, watching.

Ilse considered it, and then she nodded once. "I think it's best we speak to both of them."

If Craig Thompson had access to anesthesia and wheelchairs, then he would have to answer how his son managed to get his hands on them. Plus, *both* the Thompson men had a history where that school was concerned.

Ilse knew, her own experience with her father was possibly clouding her judgment. Right now, though, they simply needed to ask questions.

"What's this about?" Carter was insisting. His girlfriend had returned, handing a shirt through the door. He accepted it, pulling it on.

"Ma'am, you're going to need a ride home."

The girl looked nervously from Sawyer to her boyfriend. "What did he do?"

"Were you with him today?" Sawyer asked.

She gave a quick shake of her head. "I just got here."

Carter shot her a look, and she went quiet.

"Carter Thompson, we need to know if you were at the school today."

He snorted. "Of course. I have to. Part of the deal."

"What deal?"

"The deal of being a three and D wing that wants some sort of future."

"Nice to see your thinking about your future," Sawyer replied sarcastically.

Ilse frowned at Carter's hand. "Is that a cut on your wrist?"

He shifted uncomfortably. "Injury, from the last game. Small guy, big fingernails. So what?"

"We need to speak with your father too. Where is he?"

Carter scowled. "Probably at some club. He's not going to be home until late."

"I know where he is," the girl volunteered.

Carter shot her another look. "Shut up."

But she shook her head. "You said you were done with this sort of thing," she snapped. "You lied to me."

"I didn't lie about shit. They've got nothing."

The girl said, "His father's at a club downtown. It's called *Whispers*."

Sawyer said, "What's he doing at the club?"

Carter stared. "Are you dumb, man?"

"Let's say I am."

"What do you think people do at clubs? He's having a good time."

The girl muttered something beneath her breath.

Ilse leaned in, frowning. "What was that?"

Carter's girlfriend heaved a sigh. She said, a bit louder, determinedly not looking at her boyfriend, "He likes to go with much younger women. Some of them younger than me."

"And how old are you?" Ilse said.

"Eighteen. But his dad has hit on me before too."

"Sasha, Jesus, what's wrong with you? Shut up."

But Sawyer was now pulling Carter towards the vehicle. Carter shook his head, muttering something about a lawyer.

His girlfriend was still scowling on the porch. "What did he do?" she said.

Ilse was still staring at the cut along Carter's wrist. It looked like a defensive wound. She glanced towards the girl's fingernails. It didn't look like she'd been in a fight.

"Do you know how he got that cut?" Ilse said softly.

Sasha shifted. "Basketball. He told you."

"You know where he was this afternoon?"

"Hunting with his father. Like they always do after school."

Ilse stared. Sawyer paused where he had taken Carter by the car. "Say that again?" Sawyer called out.

Sasha said, "I said, they were hunting. You know, like with a license and guns. They go out for a few hours, and come back. It's perfectly legal. Is this what this is about? Carter can show you his license."

Carter was glaring at his girlfriend. "Just drop it," he snapped.

Ilse was beginning to wonder if she was making connections that didn't exist, or if they had accidentally stumbled onto something.

"Is it true you're father works in pharmaceuticals?" Ilse called down from the porch.

“So what if he does? I don’t employ him.”

“Does he give you access to any of his supplies?”

“Is this a drug bust? I didn’t do anything. You need to speak to my lawyer.”

Ilse noticed the timing of the request. She nodded to Sawyer, who helped Carter into the back of the car.

Ilse glanced at the young woman in the door. “Could you give me the name for that club again? And if you don’t mind, show me the address in your phone. Mine doesn’t do links.”

Sasha looked at Ilse as if she had just declared herself an alien. But then, with a grimace, shooting nervous glances towards where her boyfriend sat in the back of the vehicle, she pulled out her phone.

CHAPTER THIRTEEN

"You stay right there," Sawyer said, peering into the back of the vehicle.

Carter glared. "I'm handcuffed man. You think I have a choice?"

Sawyer shut the door, locked it. He glanced across the roof towards were Ilse was waiting.

"The place is loud," Sawyer said, wrinkling his nose.

Ilse shook her head, glancing towards the neon sign flashing pink and blue. *Whispers*. Giant, bold letters with light bulbs flashed around the name.

From within the club, they could hear the sound of music blaring, the tinted windows rattling, and occasionally, Ilse thought she glimpsed shapes bump against the glass.

A large man, with an even larger door behind him, glared towards the two of them. The man had a neck the size of a small tree trunk, and his arms matched.

Sawyer muttered, "You don't think there's a back entrance, do you?"

Ilse patted him on the shoulder as she moved around the hood of the car. Sawyer fell into step. Every so often, Ilse shot a glance back towards where Carter was sitting in their sedan. She couldn't quite make him out, but it appeared as if he was glaring towards them.

"Did you lock?"

Sawyer nodded. "Do you really think the dad might be in on it?"

"I don't know. But if some of the parents thought he was creeping on their daughters, it's at least worth looking into."

Sawyer and Ilse pushed through a small, golden turnstile. Decorative more than anything. Red velvet rope circled around it, creating something of a carpeted space where the bouncer stood, still glaring.

"No new admittance," the bouncer said, his eyes darting between the two of them.

"FBI," Ilse said firmly. She flashed her badge.

The bouncer scowled. "Nice try. That didn't work last week, and isn't gonna work now."

Ilse frowned. "Last week?"

He pointed at her. "You think you can get into this club without standing in line. Last week it was CIA. The week before it was local police. Before that you guys were telling me your dad owned the place."

He crossed his large arms over his inflated chest. "Now back off.

Ilse stared at him. "I'm not sure who you think I am, but I really do work with the FBI. So does he."

Sawyer flashed his badge as well.

The man in the door scowled.

Sawyer looked at Ilse for a second, waiting patiently.

She sighed, then said, "Fine, let's do it your way."

Sawyer nodded once, smiling. "Thank you," he said politely. And then he displayed his gun towards the guy in the door.

The bouncer's eyes widened, and he cursed. "Shit, wait, you're really feds?" His angry demeanor melted in an instant. He held out sausage-sized fingers as if holding them at bay. "My bad. I didn't know. I just thought, look, I don't mean any trouble. Go in. Just, don't tell anyone I let you in. If they ask, say Pedro was on shift."

He stepped aside, and Sawyer, with Ilse in tow, moved into the blaring, booming, pulsing and flashing nightclub.

Everything about the place deeply bothered Ilse on a core level.

She had never found such a dislike for any single location.

Why people considered this fun made her wonder if perhaps she was a different species. The lights alone were enough to give someone a small seizure. The smells of alcohol, body sweat, and the faint, lingering odor of puke, only combined with the obnoxious noises to remind her of one of Dante's circles of hell.

Not to mention, the music was so loud, she was deaf within seconds. Sawyer was trying to speak to her, but it didn't matter. She tapped her ears, shrugging helplessly.

Sawyer tried to yell, but even this was nearly impossible to hear.

In the end, the lanky agent settled for miming. He pointed through the audience, gesturing at the crowd, and then pointed at himself and the right side of the room. He pointed at her, and the other side.

She sighed, wincing again at another blast of music, and trying her best not to stare directly into the flashing LED lights.

The sooner she found Craig Thompson, the sooner they could get out of there.

She glanced at the small, pixilated photo she had managed to download on her dumb phone, transferring it from Sawyer's computer.

Craig Thompson looked much like his son. Pale-faced, as if he hadn't been out in the sun too much. He had an athletic physique, and was taller than average. There was something about his eyes, though, that Ilse didn't like.

Something about the way he looked into the camera on his driver's license photo. An expression that was just a bit too glib. As if he considered himself the smartest man in the room.

Ilse wasn't trying to project her own disdain for her father on another, but she was finding it difficult to separate the two.

And now, as she moved through the dance floor, her eyes darting to faces, she could feel herself getting more and more frustrated.

People bounced against each other, limbs flying, heads bobbing, drinks sloshing. She smelled more than a small amount of weed, and glimpsed pills popped as people grouped off in certain corners of the room.

Beneath the flashing lights, amidst the writhing bodies, anything seemed to go.

Ilse spotted a tall man somewhere near the middle of the dance floor. She frowned in his direction, but when he turned, she realized it wasn't Mr. Thompson.

She tried not to hold his attention for too long. When he spotted her looking, he began moving in her direction. She gave a quick shake of her head, flashed her ID, and moved on. Fortunately, this seemed to do it, and he returned to his section of the floor.

She ignored some of the smaller dancers.

On the other side of the room, weaving his way through the tide of bodies, Sawyer was also doing his best to locate their suspect.

Leaving their other suspect in the car for too long wasn't exactly protocol. But it was late. Calling backup would've taken time. And now, Ilse was determined not to waste any more of the time she had. Already Riley Sanderson had lost her life because they had been too slow.

As her eyes moved across different faces, tried not to hold eye contact for too long and communicate anything that might be distracting, she suddenly spotted a figure sitting in a small booth table at the back of the club.

She hadn't noticed at first, because the first person she'd spotted in the booth was a younger woman. She couldn't have been much older than eighteen. The woman was laughing at a joke the man had told. As

Ilse drew nearer, though, she realized the man was quite a bit older. He had leaned back, and his arms spread across the top of a red, faux-leather cushion back.

He was trying to say something else, but in the music, Ilse felt certain no one could possibly hear him.

And yet the young woman was still laughing, as if she were listening to some comedy special.

Ilse wondered how much the two of them had imbibed. Judging by the empty glasses on their table, they were not safe to drive.

She drew closer, frowning. As she circled around the stall, avoiding more dancers, her eyes settled on the man across from the young woman. He seemed tall, even sitting. And now, she realized she'd been right.

She glanced down at the pixilated photo on her phone, confirming.

Craig Thompson was grinning at a woman half his age. His hand extended across the table, grazing the young woman's knuckles. Ilse winced. She picked up the pace, pausing long enough to glance across the room and gesture at Sawyer. He was busy trying to avoid being dragged between two clearly drunk women.

When he spotted her waving him over, he let out a sigh of relief, and hastened in her direction, avoiding the tugging hands and insistent protests of the dancers.

Ilse pointed towards the man in the booth with the young date.

Sawyer frowned.

Ilse tried to speak, but her voice was lost in the buzz and blare of the horrible place.

She could feel the throbbing of the music in her stomach, like indigestion.

Sawyer approached, scowling, drawing near to the booth.

Ilse followed.

Sawyer slapped a hand on the table, and Craig Thompson looked up, frowning.

The young woman tried to speak, but Sawyer flashed his badge. The look of anger on Mr. Thompson's face quickly shifted to one of panic.

The girl was fumbling with an ID, flashing it desperately in Sawyer's direction. Though they couldn't hear each other, the intention was obvious. The girl was making it clear she was of legal age. But she was still at least twenty years younger than Craig Thompson.

Maybe this was why the women who were being abducted were

having their hair dyed. Turning young women into old ones. More age-appropriate?

The thought alone made Ilse shudder. Again, she tried not to let her own biases get in the way. Sawyer was roughly tugging at the arm of Mr. Thompson. And though he protested at first, eventually, he allowed Sawyer to drag him out of the booth.

The young woman, sitting amidst the empty drinks, looked miserable.

Ilse, holding up a finger in Sawyer's direction as he led Mr. Thompson towards the exit, approached the young woman. She pulled a small card from her wallet, placed it on the table, and pointed at the number.

A taxi service.

The girl raised her phone, wiggling it. She pointed to one of the icons on it. Ilse wasn't sure what it meant. Maybe there was something on the phone that could call a taxi as well.

She sighed, wanting to stay, to make sure the girl got home safe.

She's said, as loud as she could, "Let me get you a ride!"

But most of the words were drowned out.

The young woman hung her head, staring at one of the empty drinks.

Ilse glanced across the bar, towards were Sawyer was escorting Mr. Thompson through the door again.

Then, Ilse had an idea. She moved across the dance floor, hastening towards where the bouncer was standing by the door.

Mercifully, as she stepped out into the night, meeting the breeze, being released from the horrible, hellscape behind, she said, far louder than was necessary, "You need to make sure that girl gets home safe."

The bouncer blinked. "Me?"

"Do you see me looking at anyone else?" She said, channeling her inner Sawyer.

The bouncer shifted uncomfortably, glanced over his shoulder, through the open door, facing a blast of odor and humidity, and then nodded once. "Got it," he muttered. "I'll make sure."

"Good," Ilse said, and then she turned to follow after Sawyer where he pushed Mr. Thompson ahead towards the waiting vehicle.

CHAPTER FOURTEEN

Craig and Carter Thompson sat across the table, wearing matching expressions—equal part contemptuous but also nervous. Ilse watched where Craig's fingers tap-tap tapped against the surface of the the table. Handcuffs rattled.

"You have no right to keep us here!" Mr. Thompson snapped, waving a long finger. His son slouched in the seat next to him, scowling at the table.

Ilse settled in the chair facing the two suspects. Sawyer was already leaning back, his feet on the metal surface, crossed, his arms similarly wrapped over his thin frame. He eyed the two men with hooded eyes. This seemed to irritate Carter, who perked up, returning Sawyer's glare.

"What do you think you're looking at?" Carter snapped, leaning forward now.

Sawyer didn't say a word, but maintained the eye-contact.

Ilse sighed, deciding this meant she'd been delegated as spokesperson for the moment.

"Mr. Thompson," she said to Craig. She glanced at Carter. "Mr. Thompson," she repeated, nodding politely. "As to your earlier point, sir—we do have a right to keep you here. You were seen harassing some of the female players on your son's high school soccer team."

"That? That was months ago," snapped Craig. "I already sorted it with Sanderson."

"I'm afraid after the murder of his daughter, Mr. Sanderson has had something of a change of heart," Ilse said testily.

Her words had the intended impact.

None.

No surprise, no shock. Both of them just shifted in their chairs. Handcuffs rattled, and Carter let out a faint sigh.

"So what, he's pressing charges now?" the father said, shaking his face. His eyes were still bloodshot somewhat, and he smelled of the drinks he'd been consuming back at the club.

Ilse just watched him, allowing her silence to insist upon them.

Carter glanced at his dad. "You at *Whispers*?" he muttered.

"Not now," snapped Craig.

"Yeah—with your little trophy?"

Craig snarled at his son. "I said not now."

Sawyer interjected now. He leaned across the table. "What do you know about your father's girlfriend?"

Carter snorted. "Girlfriend? Hardly. She was his new squeeze toy. That's all. Dad's always liked 'em young. Don't you?"

"I said shut up," the father rounded on his boy. His one cuffed hand formed a fist.

Ilse leaned in her seat, preparing to intervene if necessary. But Craig's temper receded, as he seemed to remember where he was sitting. He let out a deflating sigh, leaning back and pressing his shoulders against the cold metal support of his chair.

"You arrested us because of a noise complaint from three months ago?"

"What were you two doing at that soccer game?" Ilse said, ignoring the deflection.

"My son goes to the school," Mr. Thompson snapped. "It isn't illegal to support team sports."

"It is, however, illegal to catcall underage girls, and linger on private property when you've been asked to leave," said Sawyer, his voice communicating contempt. "I don't know if you've heard of sexual harassment but we have laws against that on school property. Which, I'll add, is why you two got out of there quick. But I'm not interested in what you two did three months ago. What I want to know," Sawyer said, leaning forward, "is which one of you was there today?"

Again, neither man reacted. They were too busy, it seemed, shooting glares at each other, or trading barbs beneath their breaths. Clearly, this father-son relationship wasn't going to show up in any Hallmark movies.

Sawyer lowered his feet from the table now, leaning forward and resting his elbows on the firm surface. "Hey," he said, his voice low. "Hey!" he said louder, when his initial attempt received no reply.

The Thompsons looked over, both still frowning.

"I'm going to be honest with you," Sawyer said simply. "Normally, I'd make a pitch. Wanna hear what?"

Ilse watched, tense, certain this wasn't going any place particularly helpful. Sawyer was in one of his moods. He often got like this when young women were involved in a case. It didn't take a rocket scientist to figure out why.

Now, as her eyes darted between the pair—she wondered if her own biases were clouding her perspective. Her gaze trailed from Craig Thompson to his son, Carter.

According to the witness at the game earlier that day, only one hooded figure had been watching the girls. But the two of them had a reputation at the school. One for a sexual assault that had been covered up. Her eyes flicked to Carter.

The other for being an asshole parent that covered for his kid's crime. Not to mention a lewd creep in his own right. She glanced towards Craig.

She wondered what sort of dysfunction could ever prompt a father to take his own child to a game to harass young women.

She let out a faint puff of air, trying to keep focused, and to prevent her mind from spinning into less-than-charitable realms of consideration.

Given where she'd found the father, and the girl accompanying him, the rumors about his behavior towards some of the players were more credible than not. His day job, as a pharmaceutical salesman, also gave him access to the sorts of drugs used in the murder.

She studied Mr. Thompson closely. Then said, "Do you have access to general anesthesia?"

He'd been in the middle of complaining about the cuffs to Sawyer. But at her question, he looked over, hesitant. "Wh-what?"

"Anesthesia," Ilse repeated, crisply. "Do you have access? You work as a pharma rep, don't you?"

"Has he been sampling the supplies again?" Carter muttered.

"Shut up," snapped his father. He turned his attention back to Ilse. "What's that got to do with anything?"

"Just answer the question, sir."

"No," he said. "I don't. And also," he added, looking at Sawyer. "My girlfriend is legal age. You might not understand it, but it doesn't give you a right to harass me."

"Maybe not," Sawyer replied. "Where were you this afternoon?"

"Me? At work."

"And what about you?" Sawyer said, glancing at Carter, who'd remained mostly quiet up to this point.

The young man shifted uncomfortably in his seat. "School," he muttered.

"And after school? Did you watch the game?"

"What game?" snapped Carter. "Shit—you think one of us did

Riley, huh? I heard about it. Everyone did. The whole school's been texting."

"Not just Riley. We found her boyfriend in—"

"Yeah, heard that too," Carter said.

Sawyer snarled, "You're real broken up about it, aren't you?"

"Why should I be? I had *nothing* to do with their deaths. Neither did my dad, by the way. It's those Sandersons you should look at. Creepy couple. Just casting shade our way because they're jealous."

"Jealous of what, exactly?" Sawyer muttered.

Carter replied incoherently beneath his breath, but glanced off with a petulant jutting of his chin.

"Hang on," Craig said suddenly. "Is this... is this about those murders I saw on the news? The old ladies who were drugged?"

Ilse frowned. "Where did you hear that?"

"Online," he snapped. "I follow a crimewatch channel for the neighborhood. You think... so that's why..." he hesitated, and then his eyes widened. "Shit—no, I don't have access to anesthesia! That shit doesn't go through reps at a small pharmacy. Are you kidding me? I can show you my supply list. It's on my phone."

Ilse shot a look at Sawyer. He shrugged and then reached in his pocket, fishing out the phones they'd confiscated earlier.

It took them a moment to navigate the security code while Mr. Thompson was still cuffed, but eventually they reached the file he'd been referring to, as he directed Sawyer.

"No, dummy, *down.* Swipe *down.*"

"I heard you, this is *down.*"

"Swipe up then, to make it *go* down."

Sawyer bit his lip but held back a retort, leaning over the two men and swiping through the phone. Eventually, he stopped and tapped a finger against the glass. "This it?"

"Yeah. Open that link—it's everything."

Ilse watched Sawyer's expression.

"See?" the man said.

"What am I looking at?"

"My sales list. This is everything I have access too. Notice something?"

Sawyer shrugged.

"*No* anesthesia. Nothing like it."

Sawyer scrolled the list, his eyebrows rising. "Lot of blue pills here, Craig."

The man snorted. "I don't create the demand, I just provide the supply. If companies want it, we ship it."

"This is *everything* you sell?" Sawyer asked.

"Yeah—that's what I said, isn't it?" Craig Thompson's red-ringed eyes kept widening, then half-closing, then flinching under the glare of lights. He let out a yawn, and Ilse felt for certain she spotted a few spots of glitter stuck between his teeth.

She wrinkled her nose and looked back at Sawyer. Her partner's scowl had only deepened.

"What's your company's number?" Sawyer said.

"Shit man—I'll give you the CEO's number. He's a family friend."

"Fine—what is it?"

"Third one on speed dial. He'll be up. Give him a call. He'll vouch." Mr. Thompson sat straight-backed in his chair now, smirking towards Sawyer.

Ilse didn't like the man's expression. Too confident. Too certain. It wasn't the look of a killer backed into a corner.

Her eyes moved to Carter who was still sullenly staring off at the wall. Either of them could have been the killer. But what if she'd missed it? What if she'd let her own personal biases get in the way?

Sawyer was now walking towards the door, muttering into the phone. "My name is Agent Sawyer, sir. Apologies for the late call. But I need some information on one of your representative's product list..."

Tom's voice trailed off as he pushed out of the interrogation room, into the hall.

Craig glanced over, his sneering expression now consuming most his face. He turned this look on Ilse now. "You dragged me and my boy down here on some trumped up shit, bitch. I'm going to make you suffer."

Ilse sighed. She no longer felt so bad that perhaps she'd been a bit too eager to follow the lead towards a killer being a father-figure.

Ilse's frustration had reached new heights. She scowled across the table towards the two suspects, feeling a slow, rising sense of certainty that the alibi would check out. She turned, glancing towards the door now, rather than fixating her gaze on the Thompsons.

Her hand clenched at her side, twisting at the hem of her sweater. Vaguely, she wondered if she was wrong about this, what else had she been wrong about? Mr. Thompson was too confident. As if he knew it was going to check out. The only real connection they had between Carter and the crime scene involved the drug-supply connection.

Otherwise, all the kid stood guilty of was being an asshole.

If Ilse had made a mistake, it left her with another question... had she also made a mistake where her father was concerned?

What if he *wasn't* just sitting idly by? What if she was wrong about who had been sending the postcards, taunting her?

Faint shivers trembled up her forearms, emanating from where she kept her fist clenched around her sweater.

Ilse's heart skipped a beat, as the door pushed open again. Sawyer's expression was one of boredom.

She sighed...

He gave a faint shake of his head as he moved back into the room, already ignoring the suspects.

"Man, shit," Carter piped up. "If it matters—I was after school today. Ask Mr. Peacock."

His dad glanced over, scowling. "Detention? Again?"

"Jeez, dad, priorities."

"What for this time?"

"Forget about it!" Carter raised his voice, addressing Sawyer and Ilse. "If I was in detention, you can't pin me for something I didn't do, right? You gotta at least talk to Mr. Peacock. Old killjoy will remember me." Carter snorted at the table. "Promise."

Ilse's eyes bounced between the two suspects, biting her lip. Asshole wasn't a federal crime. Though she was starting to think it should be.

Now, she didn't even see the point in checking Carter's alibi. If the dad didn't have access to the drugs, then they were barking up the wrong tree.

Though, knowing Sawyer, they'd check everything.

Back to square one.

CHAPTER FIFTEEN

It was so funny to him, how easy it was to bluff his way onto a closed set. Even at night, *late* night, with illumination provided by floodlights set up in a sort of semi-circle.

He pushed the concessions trolley in front of him, whistling merrily as he brushed past the young, distracted intern who'd been minding the gate.

He wore a stiff, starched white jacket. He had a name tag that read *Andrew*. Which, of course, wasn't his real name.

As he moved over the asphalt, pushing his trolley laden with snacks and small water bottles, he glanced across the photo shoot.

A very attractive, brunette woman was standing in the middle of it all, waving her arms like a conductor and barking like a drill sergeant.

A small green screen had been set up for her. A miniature wooden stage served as the platform upon which she paced, back and forth, a gorgeous black dress swishing with each long-legged stride.

The director was standing next to a cameraman, watching a small screen, and making muted comments.

One of the sound technicians was fiddling with a tangle of cables beneath the edge of the stage.

He watched everything. Taking it all in.

And now, the fashion model was shouting at the sound technician for going to slowly.

He wrinkled his nose, pausing behind the director's table. He adjusted his stiff uniform, and reached down to grab a water bottle, pretending as if he were arranging the items on the cart.

No one paid attention. He had found, recently, that if you pushed something on wheels, people would pay more attention to the object than to the one pushing it.

He also had found something else out while watching television the other night.

This actress was very loud. His TV had been blaring with her voice. Even after he had reduced the volume, it had been insufferable.

And now there she was, in the person, waving her arms about, and acting as if she owned the place.

Perfect hair, perfect make up. All of it, perfect in one way or another. Flawless, symmetrical features. An athletic, toned body. And a shrill, piping voice that gave him a headache.

He could feel his anger rising with each comment she made.

More than anything, now, he wanted to shout back at her. To scream over her.

But this wasn't possible. Hadn't been possible for a very long time.

His fingers fluttered to his neck, and he massaged the skin. He winced, but then bit his lip.

The pain sometimes helped him focus. Silently watching, but also starting to move again. He maneuvered around the director, pushing the trolley in the direction of the trailers behind the large warehouse serving as the primary location. Suddenly, he heard a snapping sound.

The man turned, frowning, his eyes landing on where the director was snapping his fingers and pointing towards one of the small waters on the trolley. The man reached down, took the water and extended it towards the director.

He smiled as he did, receiving not so much as a head tilt in his direction. The director grabbed the water, twisted the cap and returned his attention to the computer screen in front of him.

The man with the trolley couldn't help but approve of the director's style. Communicating without words, quietly, direct.

He nodded. This man would live long...

But the woman on the stage?

He felt his blood boiling as he shoved the trolley ahead of him, hastening rapidly in the direction of the trailers. He'd wait for her in her dressing room. And then... he glanced at the trolley, smiling.

The perfect size, in the under-compartment, for stowing a body.

Today was going to be a very good day.

CHAPTER SIXTEEN

Ilse had never much liked squares, nor the number one. Combining the two was beginning to get very old. And yet that's where they found themselves, smack dab back at the start. The Thompsons were still being held on suspicion of soliciting minors, but this charge, even, looked unlikely to stick.

Ilse shifted uncomfortably, watching where Sawyer leaned against the wall, speaking on the phone. Foot traffic in the police station had long since decided that *avoiding* this hall, for the moment, was the better route to take. Sawyer's voice was getting louder now, and he stalked up and down outside the closed interrogation room door.

"Right now," Tom was saying. "In my guest suite. Yes—he's under arrest. For what? For *what*?" Sawyer glanced at Ilse, shrugging once, his expression not at all matching his tone.

Ilse mimed swallowing something then winced.

Sawyer tried it. "Potentially sampling the supplies, which of course is why we're calling you. No—no the son accused his father. Now listen, we're not asking much. Just a small list."

Sawyer waited now, and Ilse stared nervously like a sports fan during the last few minutes of an important match. It had been Ilse's idea to use the in they now had with the pharma company to fish for information.

It wasn't like they had much in the way of *other* options.

"I'm not *saying* it's going to impact the company," Sawyer spoke into the phone, doing his best not to sound convincing at all. "I mean... I mean it *could.* Right? I'd hate for that to happen. Yes, yes Jen we'd *both* hate for that to happen. So why don't you help us out?"

Ilse leaned in, sensing the phone call was finally shifting. Sawyer beamed now. "Yes, wonderful. Information on all paralytics would be wonderful. We need to know who has access, though, Jen. We're talking doctors, vets, nurses, clients, pharmacies. The whole shebang. Mhmm. No—no this won't come back to you. Thank you for your cooperation."

Sawyer dropped the phone and gave a little fist pump.

"Good news?" Ilse guessed.

"Good call, doc. Really good call," Sawyer said, shaking a finger and pointing it at her. "They're sending the information over. They distribute to most the locations in our region so... so as long as the killer isn't making this shit in the lab or whatever, we should get some clue where he's getting the stuff."

Ilse nodded, feeling a jolt of excitement. She could still hear muffled voices through the door as the Thompson family lawyer spoke with her clients.

Ilse shook her head, doing her best to pretend as if she weren'tr trying to listen.

"I'm thinking," Sawyer said, wagging his phone the same way he had his finger earlier, "that we get that information and try to cross-reference it with anyone who might have had a criminal past."

"Do you think that information will be easy to get?"

"I dunno. Worth checking though." Sawyer glanced at his phone impatiently. "Just hoping they send it along quick and don't make me call them again. I've never much liked being put on hold."

Ilse shifted, studying the small digital clock over the door now. The numbers shifted from 11:21 to 11:22.

It was late. Very late. The fact that a lawyer had been willing to come out this late, suggested that Mr. Thompson and his son came from means. Or at least had access to resources.

But Mr. Thompson's supplier had been clear. He didn't have access to any substance that might have been used in the murders.

Carter's teacher, who'd been up due to the constant coordination between school officials over the tragedy, hadn't enjoyed the phone call, but had confirmed that the younger Thompson had indeed been in detention right before the murders had taken place.

As much as she hated it—the two Thompsons were innocent. The new list provided by the pharma company would have to supply a new lead.

Sawyer's phone buzzed, and he glanced down, suddenly scowling. "Shit," he said. "They say it's going to take until morning to get me that information. Dammit."

Sawyer raised his phone, and Ilse heard the faintest sound of a dial tone attempting to connect.

Sawyer cursed again, and glanced towards Ilse with a helpless shrug. "It *is* getting late," he murmured, but she could tell he was frustrated.

She nodded once. "Might be good to retire for the night."

Sawyer dragged a hand across his face, emitting a loud groan. His green eyes flashed beneath the brim of his baseball cap. He shook his head, and muttered to himself, then said, you want to drive back to the city?"

All this talk of late nights, seemed to be affecting her subconscious. She stifled a yawn. She glanced again at the clock. Nearly midnight. Did she really want to make the two hour drive back to her apartment?

"Do we have a place lined up?" she said.

"We could. Shouldn't be an issue." Sawyer rubbed at his eyes, then shook his head. "I'm not driving back. I want to be here in the morning."

Ilse thought this made sense. She shifted, glancing at Sawyer, and allowing her mind to wander. He hadn't brought up his proposition back in the break room again. And he had pretended like it hadn't happened. She wasn't sure what to think of it. Wasn't sure how to best approach turning him down gently.

Because she had to turn him down, didn't she?

She didn't have the dating experience Sawyer did.

Didn't have divorce in her rearview mirror. She was entirely inexperienced.

Ilse's fingers tapped nervously against her thigh, feeling the soft material of her trousers. She glanced at the clock again. And then, with a final curse, jamming his phone angrily into his pocket, Sawyer said, "Let's go find a motel."

As he brushed past her, true to form, he called over his shoulder, "Don't worry. Separate rooms."

Instantly, she felt the blood rush to her cheeks.

He sauntered away, without so much as a glance back. She frowned after him. And then, muttering darkly to herself, she moved away from the sealed, interrogation room door. The muffled voices left in her wake.

CHAPTER SEVENTEEN

Morning sunlight flashed across Ilse's eyes, rousing her, and reminding her just how flimsy the motel mattress had been.

More like a prisoner's cot.

She shifted uncomfortably, letting out a faint groan as the lower portion of her back protested the movement. She propped on an elbow, wincing, blinking the needles of sunlight creeping through the open blinds. She had left the window uncovered intentionally, hoping to rouse at dawn.

But now, as she listened, and blinked, her eyes experiencing some small discomfort, she realized it had not been the sun that woke her. Rather, it was the faint, but insistent knocking on her door.

"Yes?" she called.

"Ilse," Sawyer said, his tone urgent.

She perked up, frowning. She pushed the blankets off her legs, and quickly left her bed, sliding onto the floor. She reached for her clothing, movements rushed.

"One moment," she said. "Did you get that information from the pharmacy?"

"Ilse, hurry up," Sawyer said. "They found another body."

He was no longer tapping insistently against the door. The silence lingered between the two of them, separated only by the thin, flimsy piece of wood. Ilse cursed, glancing back towards the uncomfortable bed, and then at the open blinds to the window.

"When?"

"Just got the call. Looks like she was killed last night."

"Same MO?"

"Looks like. I'll be waiting in the parking lot. Hurry up."

Ilsepulled on her sweater, and adjusted her sleeves. She glanced quickly around the small motel room, wishing she had brought a change of clothes. Wishing, even more, she had brought a toothbrush. The complementary mints would have to serve.

But even these were stale, she realized, as she hastened to the door, savoring the chalking texture.

Another murder. *Another* one. Which meant, he had killed three people in one day.

They were falling behind. Agent Rawley had made it clear. This was a very important case.

But they were failing, and Ilse couldn't help but feel as if it were her fault. She was distracted. Thinking about her father. About him roaming free in Germany. Thinking about Sawyer, asking her on a date. Stupid reasons to let people die. She grit her teeth in frustration, biting through one of the minutes. After final cursory check of the motel room, making sure she hadn't left anything behind, Ilse picked up her pace, shoving through the door, and hastening down the cramped, motel hall.

***

Ilse stood on the platform at the train station, scowling towards forensics milling on the tracks. Police officers guarded the exits to the station, keeping pedestrians and early morning commuters out. But Ilse couldn't help but feel a twisting sensation in her stomach, that someone should have seen something.

So how come there were no witnesses? How come no one seemed to spot anything where this guy was concerned?

Sawyer was leaning over the edge of the platform, staring at the tracks. Ilse watched where her partner engaged in discussion with one of the forensics team members. She spotted the wheelchair, marked by a small yellow evidence tag. The thing had been toppled. But it was nothing compared to the woman who'd been pushed on the tracks.

Sawyer was waving her over now, and Ilse approached with some haste.

"They found identification," Sawyer said, his voice grim. Sawyer handed Ilse a small, plastic card inside an evidence bag.

Ilse frowned. "Regina Lopez. Why do I know that name?"

"Actress. She's on those commercials with all the fireworks."

Ilse bit her lip. "This is her? He killed a celebrity?"

"I wouldn't say she was a celebrity. But she was known locally. Maybe that's why he targeted her."

Ilse shook her head in disbelief, feeling a jolt of frustration. The killer kept escalating. Killing multiple at the same scene, and now targeting high profile individuals. It was as if there was no one he couldn't reach. No one safe.

Ilse refused to glanced down at the tracks, where a couple of the forensics team were participating with a coroner's assistant to recover remains.

She turned away, glancing across the empty train station.

She spotted where three figures were waiting nervously. A man with large glasses and a flat hat, a woman carrying two cups of coffee, the steam rising and obscuring her features every couple of seconds, and, next to the two of them, was a larger man. He was wiping at his forehead and muttering numbly beneath his breath. Every so often, he addressed the officer who had been assigned to babysit them but the officer kept shaking his head and pointing in the direction of Sawyer and Ilse.

Veering off from where Sawyer was examining the identification, Ilse moved towards the three figures.

"Are these the witnesses?" she said hurriedly, glancing at the officer.

The cop nodded once.

"I didn't witness anything," said the nervous man, with the sweaty brow. "I need to get out of here. I have an important meeting this morning."

"I'm very sorry to inconvenience you," Ilse said, nodding politely. For some reason, she was relieved to have her back facing the train tracks. She said, "Do you mind telling me what you *did* see?"

"Same as them," the man said, nodding towards the other witnesses. "A man with a hood, pushing a wheelchair with an old lady. He shoved her right onto the tracks. We all saw it."

Ilse frowned. "And when was this?"

"About an hour ago. The guy with the hood bolted. No one was really paying attention to him. We were trying to help her but he'd waited until the train was coming."

Ilse glanced at the woman with the two cups of coffee.

She was nervously sampling both of them and shaking her head every so often. She let out a satisfied sigh after a particularly long sip, but then said, "Same for me. I saw him push her, then run. And then I went to see if I could help. But it was too late. The train couldn't stop in time." She bit her lip, shaking her head. "Absolutely awful. I'm going to have to go back to counseling for this, I don't doubt it."

"Again, I am very sorry," Ilse murmured. "Did you notice anything about the victim?"

Both men said, quickly, "She was gorgeous. Her hair was gray, but she looked almost like that actress," said the one with the flat hat. He snapped his fingers, wincing as he tried to remember. "Oh, you know. Those commercials with the bright lights."

Ilse nodded. "Did you notice anything else?"

All three heads shook side to side.

Ilse felt her chest tighten. "Did any of you see *anything* at all about the killer?"

Another synchronized shake of all three heads.

Now, Ilse resisted the urge to heave a sigh of her own. How was the killer avoiding detection? She glanced around the ceiling, looking for cameras. But none were visible. She made a mental note to ask Sawyer if they could contact a manager to look for a security feed. But she wasn't counting on it. The killer had been very careful so far. No one seemed to be able to find out much about him.

She watched as Sawyer moved towards her, glancing at his phone.

She gave a quick nod towards the officer with the three witnesses and said, "Thank you very much. Please leave your names and numbers in case we have more to ask." And then, she turned on her heel, facing Tom.

He came to a halt in front of her, and in a low voice, said, "It sounds like she was abducted from her trailer on a ad shoot."

"When? This morning?"

Sawyer frowned until his brow wrinkled. "That's the strange part. She was taken last night. The director and some of the crew thought she had just gone out to have some fun but when she didn't come back, they called the police. That was early this morning. Hours ago."

"So the killer took her, and kept her overnight. That's ominous."

"Everything about this is creepy. But that's what it sounds like. Yes."

"So what next? Our witnesses don't seem to remember anything. They didn't get a good look at the guy. He was wearing a hood."

"I already asked the director and the crew to stay on set. They didn't sound too happy about it. The director was talking about heading back to California but, for now, they're in place. I figure they might be a good group to talk to."

Ilse nodded. She turned to look back at the tracks, watching forensics and the coroner's assistants do their jobs. She bit her lip, and said, "He's killed five people now, Tom. Five."

"I know. I've been counting."

"Has Rawley contacted you?"

Sawyer shook his head. "I blocked his number."

"Tom!"

Sawyer shook his head. "He's insufferable. Let it go. Come on, we're not going to have anything here until they're done on the tracks. Maybe someone saw something at the ad shoot. It was supposed to be a closed set."

"You think the killer was employed by the advertising company?"

"Maybe. Doubt it. But worth checking out."

The two of them moved away, heading back towards the glimpse of sunlight at the top of the stairs leading to the exit.

CHAPTER EIGHTEEN

Ilse watched closely as the director paced back and forth on a small wooden stage. A cheap green screen hung half-removed behind him as he directed some of the interns to slowly pack certain items into large, metal storage boxes.

The man wore sunglasses and had a pen tucked behind one ear. In one hand, he gripped a script which he waved about, displaying red ink marks all up and down the page.

"No, no!" he was speaking into a bluetooth earpiece. "That won't do—it won't! She's too fat! Get me someone else."

Sawyer stood to the side of the director, watching the man with a faint frown. He cleared his throat for the second time in as many minutes.

The director sighed, tapping a finger against his earpiece. "What was your name again?" he said, glancing at Tom.

"Agent Sawyer," Tom said, emphasizing the first word.

"Right, right—Angie, look," the director said, facing Tom now and pointing a finger. "I don't have the time to discuss this. I've got to fly back home, stand in front of a board room full of piranhas, then pull down my pants and let them start feasting. Understand?"

Sawyer looked as if he distinctly did *not* understand.

Ilse felt confident she didn't *want* to understand.

Tom, not to be derailed by the vibrant image, said, "I'm afraid I can't let you fly out until you answer some questions, sir." "let me? *Let* me? What is this, nineteen forties Germany?"

Sawyer didn't miss a beat. "I mean... have you seen the architecture?"

Ilse shifted uncomfortably as the director snorted, and lowered the script he'd been waving about, fanning the air. "No, not her either!" the man said, tilting his sunglasses. "Because! She slept with Maurice—why do you think!"

Sawyer reached out, and before Ilse could stop him, he plucked the bluetooth device from the director's ear. "Mosquito," Sawyer said quickly, rubbing the device on his shirt. "Sorry about that. Didn't want you to get bitten."

The director blinked. Stared at the device in the agent's hand, then glanced up again, emitting a long sigh. "Angie, really? Alright, all I know is that I thought she'd flaked on us. We agreed on an early call time. But she wasn't at the hotel. You may not know this," he said, with a tilt of his eyebrows, "But Lopez was known for being a bit of a diva."

Ilse leaned in now. "And did anyone show hostility for her around the set? Did anyone dislike her?"

"Yeah. Me. And the head of makeup, and that guy over there. Hey, guy, what's your name?" One of the interns tearing down the green screen blinked. "Uh... Glen?"

"Glen didn't like her either, did you Glen?"

"Umm..."

"See?" the director finished, turning back with a significant tilt of his eyebrows.

"And what was the reaction when everyone heard the news?" Ilse soldiered on, blinking sunlight as the second half of the green screen dropped and the sun flashed through.

"Reaction? I mean... shock? Awe? Horror... Do you know how much money I'm losing? Shit—we also did something of a life insurance thing with most our talent last year. That's going to be a real kick in the nuts."

"Did anyone see her leave?" Tom said, crossing his arms. "Hey—hey Gary!"

Glen looked over.

"You were watching the gate last night, yeah? Did you see Lopez leave?"

Glen shook his head. "I—I... no, sir. Didn't."

"Did anyone come or go that didn't belong on set?" Ilse called to the intern.

The young man sighed, brushing hair from his eyes and lowering a black pole he'd been attempting to screw free from the main frame. "Not that I could tell. But I've only been on set a couple of weeks. A lot of people come and go. Makeup... interns. Concessions."

"Do you remember what they looked like?" Ilse said. "What about the interns?"

"I mean... I know Wanda," he said, pointing to a young woman with dark braids wrangling a metal suitcase.

"What about concessions? Who was that?"

He shook his head, though. "I really couldn't say. Everything was... was..." he glanced towards the director then looked away again. "Sort of high strung, you know? I was focused on the stage. Shit. I'm sorry."

Ilse forced a quick, reassuring smile, then turned her attention to the set. She spotted six people near the stage. And another four by the trailers. By the look of things, three more figures were moving near the front of a warehouse, watching the FBI agents with curiosity.

"Right," she said. "You can't think of anyone... wearing a hood, maybe?" she said, wincing sheepishly.

Glen shook his head. "Not that I remember."

"So no one saw Lopez leave?" Sawyer asked. "She was the famous one on set, right? You would've noticed."
The director bristled at this comment, but Glen shrugged. "I guess not."

Sawyer glanced back at Ilse. "But we *know* she left, yeah?"

Ilse sighed. She returned her attention to the director who's hand was creeping towards the bluetooth device Sawyer had confiscated.

"Could you describe Ms. Lopez to us?" Ilse said, hesitating. "Was she... athletic?" Ilse winced, then tried. "Did she... maybe help dress hair?"

The director stared at her. He paused, inhaled, paused, then said, "Are you... are you quite sure you're FBI?"

"Just answer the question," Ilse said testily.

The director shook his head. "I mean... what's there to say? She was a walking cliché. Everything had to be done her way. Makeup, wardrobe, schedule. Shit. She even asked me not to wear my green tie. I love that tie. She was outgoing too, though. Fun to be around when she wasn't in one of her moods."

Ilse stared, trying to process the information while also thinking back to their first two victims. One of them an outgoing hairdresser. The other a door to door salesman. The last one a soccer star.

And now an actress?

Was the killer targeting successful women?

No... no that wasn't it. The first two women were clearly successful in their own right, but not the same way a fashion model was...

"He's targeting alphas..." Ilse said slowly, shifting. "I... I hate using that word. But—but what if..." She glanced at Sawyer, tilting her head inquisitively.

"Alphas?" He asked, turning his back on the director and allowing him to retrieve his bluetooth device. The man hastened away, quickly reconnecting his call as he went.

"I mean... Think about it. A soccer star who was playing a game. A hairdresser who was outgoing, gregarious and overly talkative. A door-to-door saleswoman who's *job* it was to talk to strangers and be outgoing. And now..." Ilse waved a hand towards the stage they were standing on.

Sawyer glanced at his feet where they spread at shoulder width on the wooden surface. He then looked slowly up.

"Shit... you think so?"

Ilse shrugged. "I mean... At the very least, he doesn't seem to like extroverts, does he?"

Sawyer sighed. "Dammit... Why didn't I notice that earlier?"

"I didn't either."

Sawyer tilted his cap and stared off for a moment. He looked back at her, frowning. "So now what?" he said. "What's the call, doc? We can't exactly search the database for *extroverts.* Why? Why's he targeting them anyway?"

Ilse hesitated, considering this second question first. She often tried to put herself in the mind of a killer, seeing things from their perspective. It wasn't a very *enjoyable* experience, but it helped her on the job. It helped with her clients.
The why mattered.

So what sort of person targeted athletic, successful, outgoing women?

A chauvinist? No... no... that form of contempt was usually reserved for females in business suits. In fact, Ilse doubted that a *hairdresser* or a *fashion model,* stereotypically female roles, would upset someone motivated by sexism.

So if not that, then what?

Ilse let out a faint sigh. She couldn't be certain. Not yet. There simply wasn't enough information.

"Think we should... maybe look into any police reports?" she said suddenly, glancing at Tom.

"You think our killer targeted Lopez before?"

"I mean... she was something of a celebrity. People like that always have stalkers. Some sort of hang-ons. It's worth a shot. Maybe our killer was noticed... He clearly studies his victims before he attacks."

Sawyer nodded. "Yeah. Fine. Give me a second. I'm going to grab a water."

She watched as Tom moved in the direction of a small concessions table against the corrugated metal wall of the warehouse.

She frowned... Didn't Glen say that someone from concessions had come through with a trolley? So why did they have a table as well?

Ilse let out a faint sigh... Had the killer come in disguise?

She'd asked Glen about the caterer. He hadn't remembered a thing. Why was this a commonality? How come no one seemed to remember anything about this guy? What made him so forgettable?

As Sawyer moved towards the concessions table, she turned towards the director. There were cameras rolling on set, when Lopez had been there, weren't there? Test-footage and B-roll was often shot at wider angles.

Maybe one of them had spotted something.

CHAPTER NINETEEN

The camera footage showed nothing except the set itself. And the director had gone out of his way to make sure no one put themselves in the shot. Behind her, Ilse heard the director muttering as the film played again. "See," he said. "Nothing—now... how much longer are you going to be here?"

"You can leave," Sawyer snapped. "Just leave the trailer."

The director shook his head, pushing through a metal door and stepping back out onto the asphalt. As he departed, the door slowly shut behind him, leaving Ilse and Tom alone once again in the small trailer.

The flickering screen displayed the scene from the set the day before, and Ilse watched it on repeat.

She wrinkled her nose. "I always thought those fireworks were *real.* Huh."

"Movie magic," Sawyer muttered. "What about this one?" he said suddenly, staring at his phone. The glow from the device competed with the glow of the viewing screen. "Guy stalked her three months ago. Kept saying they were meant to be together. When she called the police, he broke down weeping and—ah, shit. Never mind. That was in Colorado."

"What is that, six?" Ilse asked, glancing towards Sawyer, subsequently reaching out and turning off the flickering television screen.

"Seven," Tom said. "Man—I'm really glad I'm not a pretty lady. I can't imagine having this many weirdos stalking me." He shook his head. "You must have had your own experience with that, yeah?"

He said it noncommittally, as if there was nothing odd about the assumption, and yet Ilse felt distinctly uncomfortable at the comment.

She did *not* consider herself a particularly pretty woman. She went out of her way *not* to attract too much attention. And yet Sawyer was once again studying his phone, completely unaware—it seemed—that he'd said anything irksome. It wasn't that she didn't sometimes *think* about maybe... one day... just considering...

But no. No, she knew that wasn't a path she could take.

People would only get hurt if she drew near to them. Besides, it wasn't like Sawyer really meant it, anyway. He was probably just trying to be funny.

She shifted uncomfortably, uncertain how to respond. In the end, she decided not to. She still hadn't summoned the nerve to turn down his date request. And now, more than ever, she felt the discomfort of the close proximity in the dark room, standing a bit too close for comfort.

She hated this part.

When people showed interest, overt interest, it changed things.

She'd always sort of *known.* Or at the very least *suspected* there might have been some attraction. Maybe...

Maybe even...

Mutual? She shifted uncomfortably, brushing nervously at her hair and flicking it past her ear.

"Alright... hang on," Sawyer said. "Finally—a local guy. He's... yeah, shit—Seattle."

Ilse perked up, staring at her partner. Sawyer was shaking his head, muttering to himself. "I mean... looks like... Could be." Then he suddenly clicked his tongue. "There we go. Hear this, doc." He cleared his throat similarly to the way Lopez had done on the movie screen before reciting her lines. "Looks like this creep used a fake police complaint to get near her. Took her to court—ha, the gall!"

"Took her to court?"

"Or... no, tried to. It got thrown out. When they dug a bit deeper, it turned out the guy was trying to get near Ms. Lopez. He had something of an obsession. Some real creepy online search traffic too. Erotic stories about her. Deepfakes."

"Deep what?"

"Trust me—you don't want to know. Our guy's name is Pierre Toman. He lives about an hour from here... What are the odds he hears about the shoot on the internet and it gets his gears, going, you know?"

"If he's obsessed with Lopez, why target the other women?"

Sawyer exhaled faintly, but then went still. "Ah—look at this."

Ilse leaned in. But before she could read it, Sawyer narrated for her.

"Looks like Mr. Toman used a *noise* complaint to try and sue Ms. Lopez. He lived near enough one of her last locations that he claimed the soundtrack they were using was too loud. Sued for damages because he..." Sawyer trailed off, shaking his head. "Something about losing a job, or whatever. But that's interesting, isn't it? A noise ordinance complaint? Isn't that what you were saying about the victims, that our killer envies their liveliness?"

"I... I mean I didn't say that *exactly.* But it... it does fit."

Ilse frowned. "So how come they looked so closely at this guy? Is it usual to criminally investigate a noise complaint?"

"No..." Sawyer's tone went suddenly sharp. "It is, however, when the guy making the complaint is slated for a criminal trial."

Ilse looked over sharply. "What sort of trial?"

"Date rape allegation. Victim—unnamed—claims Mr. Toman offered her a drink with tranquilizers in it, but her friend warned her in time. Trial was set for next month." Sawyer looked at Ilse, eyes wide. "What if that's why he snapped? He knows he's going away for a while, so he's taking shots at women while he still can. Tranquilizers... Maybe he's doing creepy stuff before—"

"There was no sign of sexual assault on the other victims," Ilse cut in.

"No... no but maybe he just gets off on the power trip."

"I... so he was harassing Ms. Lopez, made a noise complaint and had a trial set for attempted date rape with tranquilizers." Ilse frowned, shaking her head. "Where is he now?"

"Looking it up as we speak. I think we need to pay Mr. Toman a visit."

CHAPTER TWENTY

"Of course," Ilse muttered. "Of *course* he's a park ranger. Why is it always park rangers?"

"It's... is it?" Sawyer glanced at her from the driver's side, pulling slowly into a dirt parking lot under the swaying trees.

Ilse shook her head. "An address should be a house. Should have windows. Or a door. It shouldn't be a hundred thousand bloody acres."

Sawyer snorted. "What's got in your bonnet?"

Ilse shook her head, muttering darkly as she pushed open the passenger-side door and stepped into a cloud of slowly dissipating dust kicked up by the rubber wheels.

She waved a hand in front of her face, clearing the air and wincing, blinking against the grains threatening her eyes. Behind her, she watched as two more police vehicles approached, crunching over the gravel entry.

Sawyer gestured at the officers to join the two of them by the trailhead. It was still early in the morning, on a weekday, which meant only a few other cars were parked in the lot. One, where a woman was attempting to unload a stroller. The woman glanced at the cops, frowned, and slowly closed the door to her car, ushering a small child hastily back into the vehicle.

Sawyer shifted, gesturing at the officers and calling out, "We'll be checking every one of Mr. Toman's areas. Make sure to leave no stone unturned." Sawyer glanced towards a pile of rocks at the trailhead. "Not literally," he added. "You two head down the east trail. You two stay here, and keep an eye on the lake over there. If he comes back, radio the rest of us."

"I guess that leaves us with the north trail," Ilse murmured, glancing towards the dusty ground meandering through the trees. A thick chain between two brown, metal posts blocked any traffic. The trail itself narrowed as it went, framed with signs prohibiting motor vehicles.

"You good, doc?"

"I'm fine. I was just wondering what sort of ranger he is. Some of them carry tranquilizers for big game."

Sawyer hesitated, but then tapped his nose. "Not quite the same as the anesthesia the coroner mentioned."

"No, perhaps not. But it does mean he has experience with paralytics. Experience with administering them to wildlife—living things... What if this isn't the first time he's used some sort of drug to incapacitate a victim?"

And with that wonderful notion spinning through her head, Ilse set off, Sawyer at her side, moving over the metal chain, and up the trail into the forest preserve.

This wasn't the first time Ilse had gone looking through the woods with Sawyer at her side. In fact, she remembered one of the very first cases they had. At the time, she had volunteered to be used as bait. She far preferred this version, though. Sawyer serving as backup.

The thick, tangled branches arched overhead, boughs interlocking and leaves rustling against each other. At first, towards the start of the trail, the undergrowth was kept in check, neatly trimmed back. But the further they went, the more overgrown things became.

Ilse detected the faint scent of earth and all things green. Mosquitoes zipped from the trees, investigating the morsels that had wandered into their terrain.

Sawyer's hand served as a swatter, knocking the irritants out of the air.

Ilse was glad she wore long sleeves. She tugged at her sleeves, further protecting her wrists.

The tattoo on one wrist, simply read, *Take captive every thought...*

And now she was trying to do just this. Her mind kept wandering to her father in Germany but she was desperately attempting to focus.

Sawyer kept a brisk pace, which she hastened to keep stride with. He didn't slow for the smaller woman, and she didn't expect him to. Occasionally, she heard a burst of static over the radio on Sawyer's shoulder, as one of the other search parties provided updates. So far, though, no one had spotted their suspect.

Ilse continued to consider where she was missing something. What thoughts were getting in the way of solving this case?

Mr. Toman seemed like the perfect candidate. And now, she was beginning to realize why. It wasn't just that the woman he killed were loud, or successful, or significant. Something else had occurred to her. They were all healthy. All young—all, in their own way, barring one exception, quite beautiful. One had even been a fashion model. One a hairdresser. One a young athlete. The door-to-door salesman still didn't quite compute. But even this, Ilse realized made sense if she didn't focus on just *one* reason, but all of it. A sort of jealousy?

She couldn't be entirely certain. But as she moved through the woods, picking up her pace, she realized something else.

A place like this, amidst the trees and streams, and isolated bike and hike paths, was the perfect place to go for silence. Only the whisper of branches, the faint shiver of leaves. Only the sound of the wilderness around her.

Was that why Mr. Toman enjoyed the woods? Perhaps his attacks were targeting those who dared to break the silence of the forest. She hesitated, but frowned. She couldn't say she knew for certain why he did what he did.

But one thing seemed clear. The noise complaint he had made about Ms. Lopez helped point to a mind that derided cacophony.

The killer would feel at home amidst the silent trees.

She was still trying to piece together a potential behavioral explanation, when Sawyer pulled up short.

They had come to a fork in the road. One of the trails went off high, inclining towards the right, a sign suggesting that it led to an overlook. The other trail went down, moving towards a small pond, which was just visible from where they stood.

Sawyer scratched his chin. "I hate to say it," he said slowly.

Ilse sighed. She checked the shoulder mic that she'd been given connected to the radio on her belt. "I'm good," she said.

Sawyer glanced at her. "You sure?"

"I said I'm good. I'm an agent too, aren't I? Well—this is what we do..." Even as she said it, she wished she felt it with the same conviction in her tone."

Sawyer hesitated, scratched at his chin, then said, as clearly as he could, "Call... if you see anyone, *call*."

"It's going to be fine. Which one do you want?"

Sawyer shrugged. "I need the exercise." And then he began moving up the incline.

Typical Tom. No long discussion, just a rueful, sheepish shrug, and if brief apology. She didn't blame him. It made perfect sense. Time was of the essence. The killer had taken three lives the night before. They didn't have time to dawdle.

More police officers were heading their way. But it would take nearly an hour before they arrived.

The small police station of the even smaller town simply wasn't able to provide an entire search team. Besides, it wasn't likely that she would stumble upon the killer anyway. Was it? It was a big forest preserve. Then again, they had been provided a map of the ranger's route by his supervisor before setting out.

Ilse muttered nervously beneath her breath, "Fifteen victims. Brown eyes. Antisocial personality disorder..."

She trailed off, picking up the pace, and moving down the path leading to the pond. She could hear the sound of Sawyer's crunching footsteps as he moved up, away from her.

Her radio crackled. "You good, doc?" Sawyer said.

"It's been ten seconds, Tom. I'm fine."

"Just checking. How about the rest of you? How are things? See anyone?"

Ilse listened vaguely as the other officers gave status reports. No one had seen Mr. Toman yet.

Now, again, moving through the trees, she didn't have the luxury of a personal bodyguard. Sawyer made her feel safe. It was a strange thing to consider. Especially because she had never felt safe. Not once. It wasn't something she could describe to those who didn't understand trauma. Most people lived under the belief that they were invincible. Not to everything. People always had their pet phobias. But in Ilse's case, it wasn't just a phobia. It wasn't even solely trauma. It was a lifestyle in her formative years that had taught her to be scared of her own shadow. She didn't need a reason to feel terror. It simply existed. She didn't move from a place of stasis to fear, but rather lived in a place of fear, and struggled to find stasis.

Over the course of years, she had managed to walk back as much of her formative years as she could. And so it was rare to feel safe. Very rare. Usually it took more than one deadbolt lock and security camera. Usually, even that didn't help.

How often did she check door handles? Locks? She would often find herself, against her own will, shutting and closing a door three times before her mind would believe that it was properly closed. There were the strangest things that triggered her desire for protection.

Ilse gave a faint sigh, picking up the pace and leading away from where Sawyer was moving.

It was like stepping into an icy pond. The difference between walking with him and without him

She felt as if she could take care of herself but certainly didn't share Sawyer's experience in the field.

Her hand moved towards her holster, hidden just under the hem of her sweater. She buttoned and unbuttoned one of the clasps, trying to focus.

More radio chatter. More nothing. No one had seen their suspect.

Which, in Ilse's estimate, was bad news. The longer they went without finding Mr. Toman in one of the other locations, the more likely it was that he would be found near her.

She heard a noise.

And went suddenly still.

Another noise, off to her side. She turned, slowly, frowning into the woods.

"Hello?" She said, tentatively. Her finger moved towards the button on the radio, just in case.

The sound had stopped.

Shivers trembled up her spine. Now, under the thick canopy, the foliage rustling above, she could barely see the sunlight. It was as if the trees themselves had crowded out the darkness.

"Hello?" she said, louder and more insistently.

And then came the sound of heavy breathing. Footsteps. She took a wary step back, her hand on her holster, hidden just beneath her sweater.

A figure emerged from the forest now, wiping at his forehead with the back of a green uniform's sleeve. The man adjusted a baseball cap of his own, returning his bandanna to his neck. He was carrying a small saw, and—whistling—he was moving towards where an ATV had been parked. Ilse hadn't spotted it at first, the trees camouflaging the vehicle.

Now, though, as he approached the stalled ATV, he paused. Then glanced at her, his eyes widening.

"Oh, hey there," he said in a sort of drawl.

He blinked a couple more times, wiping at his face with his bandanna. He had a face like a schoolboy, but with wrinkles that ruined the deception. Middle-aged, but with boyish features. His lips were strangely pale as if he were perpetually cold.

His eyes kept moving, lingering in all the wrong places and moving again.

He had a twitchy, nervous disposition that didn't match the warmth or friendliness of his tone.

"Mr. Toman?" she said slowly.

He blinked, then grinned, pointing a finger towards a fabric nametag. "Damn, girl, you got good eyes to see from there. And what's your name?"

He turned fully to face her, his back to his ATV now, his hand clutching the saw.

She shifted uncomfortably under his scrutiny.

"You need some help?" he asked, glancing past her now. "You ain't alone are you?" He said this with a faint chuckle as if it were the least significant thing in the world. And yet the *way* he said it made her suddenly pause. She took a hesitant step back, her hand still on her holster.

"Hey now," he said, still grinning, his young features rearranging into something of a quizzical smile. "I'm just trying to help. No one's with you, sweetie? You lost in the woods? Maybe I can give you a ride, huh?"

He nodded towards the ATV.

She frowned. "Don't call me sweetie. My name is Dr. Beck, and I'm with the FBI."

He hesitated, then burst out laughing. "Ah, shit," he said, chuckling. "Sure you are... Sure, sure!" She was beginning to resent how many people didn't believe her when she told them her place of employment. Now, though, using his laughter as an excuse to step nearer, he closed the distance.

"Man, you are a sight for sore eyes," he said. "Staring at trees all day... it goes to your head." He chuckled.

She took another step back.

"Oh come on, darling," he said. "I don't bite." He winked. "Unless you want me—shit."

She lifted the edge of her sweater, showing her holster. Sawyer's same trick from back at *Whisper's.* And while she promised herself she'd never let Tom know she'd borrowed a play from his book, she felt a bit of a thrill at the sudden shift in Mr. Toman's voice and posture.

He'd been coming closer, dismissive, arrogant and clearly threatening, but one look at her weapon and he was now stumbling back, shaking his head urgently and muttering, "Ha, I'm just teasing. Happy to help you get out of here."

Now, he was pretending as if he hadn't seen the gun. Looking determinedly away from her and gesturing towards his ATV. "I work for the forest, by the way."

"I know who you are, Mr. Toman," Ilse said firmly. "Please keep your hands where I can—"

A blur of motion suddenly erupted from the side of the path. She heard a sudden grunt, followed by a quick *thump* and then an agitated cloud of dust. Tom Sawyer had come hurtling out of the trees, slamming straight into Mr. Toman.

Ilse frowned, blinked and realized she'd accidentally left her radio on, transmitting.

"Tom," she said hurriedly, rushing forward. "Tom—it's fine. I had it handled. He—oof..." She winced as Sawyer bent Mr. Toman's arm back.

"Stop struggling," Sawyer snapped. "Stay down..." Cuffs clicked into place. Gasping, and still scowling, Sawyer looked sharply at her. "You okay?"

"I'm fine, Tom. Maybe careful where you're putting your knee."

"Oh—yeah. Woops. Get up, asshole." Sawyer dragged Toman to his feet. "You like talking dirty to ladies alone in the woods? Hmm? Why don't you run a couple of your lines by me. No—I mean it. Go ahead. What were you going to do next with my partner?" Sawyer shoved Mr. Toman, pushing him back up the trail, heading in the direction they'd come from.

Ilse stopped long enough to grab Sawyer's hat where it had fallen when he'd tackled the suspect. She dusted it off on her thigh and then hasted after the two men. She couldn't help but notice that Mr. Toman had a lot less to say now that an audience had arrived.

CHAPTER TWENTY ONE

Blue and red lights flashed across the dark green forest, illuminating branches and boughs, shifting in multi-hued spotlights over the shivering leaves.

Ilse leaned against the hood of the car, peering over the door towards where Sawyer was speaking with their suspect. Mr. Toman's boyish features had creased into a petulant expression, complete with jutting lip and wide eyes. His intonation kept flitting to higher octaves, bringing to mind the cadence of the familiar phrase, "Who *me*?"

But Ilse wasn't buying it. She'd seen the look in the ranger's eyes. A predatory leer. If she hadn't had her weapon, or if Sawyer hadn't shown up, then Mr. Toman had intended to harm her. That much had been obvious.

Given her background, training on the mat, she felt as if she still might have been able to hold her own. But how many women out there, alone in the woods had encountered a similar predator, unable to defend themselves?

She could feel her fury rising now. A man like this... who'd used tranquilizers in an attempt to date rape a woman, was exactly the sort who might wheel helpless women about in wheelchairs.

Now, though, he was projecting a completely different image. A faint, pleading whine to his voice as he spoke to Sawyer. "I didn't do anything, though. This—this is what's most baffling, sir. I was just trying to help the nice little lady."

As he spoke, his wide-eyes and trembling voice attempted to communicate innocence. And yet as Ilse stared through the glass of the open car door, she knew they'd found a predator. The only question: was he *their* predator?

Definitely a creep. But was he the man hunting women throughout Washington State?

"How come," Sawyer said, his tone hard, "you've had three restraining orders against you in the last five years?"

"Wh-what?" The man blinked. "I don't remember those."

Sawyer raised his phone, reciting, "One against Regina Lopez. Another against Demi Greer. And the most recent one against Miranda

Li. In fact, you're in a pending trial over criminal charges on Miranda's behalf." Sawyer lowered his phone, his eyes hooded, his tone cold.

Nothing about Toman's charade was working on Tom. Ilse felt a flicker of gratitude for this.

"Why don't you drop the act, Tommy," Sawyer snapped. "Where were you last night?"

"Umm... Working, sir. Working."

"Don't call me sir. That right is reserved for citizens. Did anyone see you working?"

Mr. Toman raised his cuffed hands as if presenting the forest on a platter. "It's pretty lonely work, si-er... man. I don't know what you think I can prove. I didn't mean to scare your lady partner."

"Hey—hey, stop looking at her. Look at me." Sawyer snapped his fingers.

But Ilse took the askance glance as her cue. She slipped around the edge of the open door, and faced Mr. Toman, frowning.

"Did you want to rape me?" she said simply.

He stared at her, mouth gaping, blinking. Sawyer's scowl only deepened. Ilse didn't flinch. She knew the sorts of evil that people were capable of. Innuendo, inference were some of the best ways to hide what a person really was. Pretending and normalizing allowed men like this to skate.

She repeated the question, more firmly, no inch of embarrassment in her voice. If anyone ought to have been embarrassed it was Toman. "Did you want to rape me?" she said more firmly. "Is that why you started walking towards me? Making innuendos? Calling me inappropriate names? Is that what you did with Ms. Li? Is that what you hoped to do with Ms. Lopez?"

Now, Toman was having a hard time keeping his performance. Wide-eyes and lilting tone didn't much match with such accusations. He seemed caught in an impasse. He shifted uncomfortably, shaking his head, pausing, wincing, then shaking it again.

"I don't know what you're talking about," he said breathlessly.

"And what about Erin Pratt?" Ilse said quickly. "Riley Sanderson? What about Tiffany Perkins? Do you know what I'm talking about with them? Or are you still playing possum, Toman?" Ilse didn't let him answer. She wasn't trying to get answers yet. She was trying to rattle him. To confront him with the ridiculous juxtaposition between who he was and who he was pretending to be. Often times, performances vanished when a bright enough spotlight shone on them.

"Alright, how about I help you?" Ilse said simply. "You targeted vulnerable women and got off on hurting them. Is there something about strong women you don't like? Is it how they make you feel, *sir*?"

Now, she could see the anger in his eyes. There it was. This was the spark she'd been looking for. It was hard to disguise hatred, contempt when confronted with the object of your hatred. He was staring at Ilse with a fury in his gaze. He kept trying to wobble his lip, stare doe-eyed about the parking lot of the forest preserve, but now, every so often, his eyes flashed.

Sawyer had gone quiet, watching closely, allowing Ilse to work. Still, she noticed how he'd shifted, nearly imperceptibly, placing himself between her and the suspect.

She felt a flash of gratitude, but also reached out and gently pushed him to the side. Sawyer allowed her to guide him to the left, giving Ilse a clear line of sight of Mr. Toman.

Her eyes met his. Contempt met shrewd frigidity.

"You don't know what you're talking about, lady," Toman said. But now it was more sneer than placation.

"Why don't you enlighten me," Ilse murmured. "I'm very interested in what you have to say... Do you often accost women in the woods? How many victims, Toman? Is this the first time you've killed?"

He wrinkled his nose and snorted. "Killed? What are you talking about."

But there was panic in his voice. She saw it now. So did Sawyer. Tom was leaning in, his thumb on his right hand hooked through his belt.

"I think you know," Ilse said quietly. "Why did you kill them?"

"Them?" now he snorted though. "There's no *them*."

Sawyer shifted. Ilse, though, frowned. She studied Mr. Toman. The wind was picking up from the trees, the leaves brushing boughs and branches. The rustling sound of the forest seemed like a sudden eruption of faint whispering. All of nature witnessing the strange spectacle in the parking lot. Ilse tried not to allow the rising breeze, the blinking sunlight, the murmur of voices behind her, or the flash of police lights to distract her.

She said, slowly, "Not *them.* So *her*? Why did you kill her?"

He stared at her now. His face lost its color, the blood leaving his cheeks and chin. The latter portion of his visage trembled as he tried to speak. He let out a faint little huff of air. "I—I don't know what you're talking about," he muttered.

Sawyer snorted. "Come on, Toman... Really? This is how you want to play it? You're not little Red Riding Hood, bud. You're the damn wolf. Own it. Be a man, and own it."

"I don't know... don't know what you're..."

"Did you rape her too?" Ilse said. "Is that what you like doing? Is that fun for you? Is it because no one will have you otherwise? You do look very, very young," she said, slowly, meticulously, like a surgeon with a scalpel. Ilse, knowing people, had spent a great deal of time getting to the bottom of most of her clients' worst fears and deepest insecurities. It felt wrong to use such a thing against a man. But then again, she could still see the predatory look in his gaze as he'd encroached on her in the woods.

Now, she could see the guilt scrawled across his face. A confession in the back of a police car was far better than the usual way these cases ended. Men who killed often knew their futures weren't bright. It was why spree killings ended in suicide by cop, or otherwise.

And yet here was an opportunity to end without further violence.

And so Ilse used her knowledge of the human mind—specifically, human insecurity, to go on the attack for a change.

It felt odd, almost *icky*. But she didn't back down.

"I can see the way you look at me, Toman. Who was it? A highschool girlfriend? No—no, younger. Must have been in grade school... Something humiliating, I'm guessing? Did a girl lead you on just to mock you? I'm guessing it doesn't help that you still look like a fifth-grader, does it? Women, true women don't want to be with a child. And that's what you are. Your face, your attitude, your personality... You're just a child trapped in a man's body. No one would *want* to be with you. So you force them, don't you? That's what's fun for you, but when you secretly look at your choices, late at night, you hate yourself... And so that hatred comes out on others. Because," Ilse said, pressing, her tone still cold, meticulous, "you don't have the damn *balls* to admit the real problem. You. You're the problem. Not women. Not everyone else. You're the problem. Aren't you? Say it, Toman. You're the problem. You're not dateable. No one would want to be with—"

"SHUT UP, BITCH!" he screamed suddenly, the emotions bursting from his lips, his eyes bugging like some ghoul. "You think I couldn't make you squeal, too, huh? Yeah? You think you're some big shot? Hiding behind a man?" He was shaking now, his face red all of a sudden, his jaw trembling. He was glaring at her, nostrils flaring as he inhaled and exhaled in deep breaths. He started chuckling now, fully immersing in this new role he'd cast for himself.

This was what killers so often did. They could never face reality. Everything was about power or control. They felt so powerless, so helpless that they projected power. They would never in a million years, without help, admit to their own sense of inadequacy. Powerlessness.

Now, he was just spluttering, shaking his head, projecting power. Like a puffer fish.

Truly powerful men, though, controlled their emotions.

This was just an actor playing the part.

"I could've had some fun with you, yeah?" He laughed, guffawing, though there was no humor in his voice. "You think you know me? You think you got me? I didn't kill that one whore. What? I'm guessing you found here beneath the storage locker? Whatever—who cares. She's gone. I did that. Me!" He jutted his chin, shaking his fists together where they clamped over the cuffs, like some sort of Olympian celebrating a victory. "Not just her, neither. Bet you can't find the others." He laughed, winking. "No—no you can't."

Ilse listened to this, frowning slowly. He was admitting to a murder...

But not...

Not the *right* murders.

"Erin Pratt?" Ilse said slowly.

"I don't know the whore's name, lady. I didn't ask for yours either, did I? That's the fun. Pure anonymity. My daddy used to tell me not to name the bunny rabbits. Made it harder to eat 'em." He chuckled now, making kissing noises.

Sawyer coughed, stepped forward, and, disguising the sound with another cough, punched the man on the nose, sending him reeling back into the car.

Ilse sighed. Tom often got protective where she was concerned.

She watched Mr. Toman splutter and curse, a faint trail of blood now trickling down his upper lip. Sawyer slammed the door shut, cutting off any further protest. As he did, though, his hand was shaking badly.

"Sorry," he muttered beneath his breath. "Sorry," he repeated. "Sorry," he kept saying.

In his eyes, Ilse spotted the same look she'd seen back at the prison. A horrified, furious look of rage. A suppressed anger that only came out in short bursts of emotion. She wondered if this was the same Sawyer that had punched Rawley in his office all those years ago, earning himself disciplinary leave and a transfer.

Now, though, Tom's face was pale. His voice shook with concealed emotion. "I should've said something sooner. Shouldn't have let him talk to you like that."

"It's fine, Tom," Ilse said softly, patting her partner on the arm. "It's fine. I've heard worse. Trust me. Far worse."

He let out a rattling breath, looking her dead in the eyes. "That makes me even angrier. You shouldn't *have* to hear worse. That's not... *shit.*" He pressed his back against the glass of the car as if intentionally concealing the suspect from view.

"So," Sawyer said quietly. "Guess we have our guy. He basically admitted to murder."

Now, though, as Sawyer calmed and he massaged his knuckles, Ilse glanced towards where some of the other police were moving back down the trails, or investigating the ATV, along with Mr. Toman's belongings. She frowned, then gave a faint shake of her head.

"No," she said simply.

"No, what?"

"It's not our guy," she murmured. "He's a murderer. A predator. But not our predator."

Sawyer frowned now, shoulders shifting against the glass. He crossed his arms over his thin chest. "How do you mean?"

"I mean," she said simply, "It's not our guy, Tom. He admitted to a murder. To attacking women. According to his record we know that. But he never even mentioned our victims. He didn't recognize their names."

"Yeah—yeah but you heard him, doc. He doesn't know their names because he doesn't ask. He's a pervert. A weirdo."

"But he *did* know Ms. Lopez' name," Ilse said simply. "He targeted women in the woods. He liked the isolation, the privacy. Look at him, Tom. He's a coward. Motivated by lust and inadequacy. Our killer... he wheels his victims around in *public.*"

"While they're drugged. While he's in full control."

"Yes... but it's not the same thing."

Sawyer tugged at his brim. "Shit... I think you're wrong, doc. But... I mean, if not Toman, who?"

"I... We should tell the police to check beneath the supply shed he mentioned. I'm guessing there's a body hidden there."

"Just because he admitted to *another* murder, doesn't mean he's not guilty of these ones."

Ilse hesitated, brushing at her hair and shifting uncomfortably in the dusty parking lot. She glimpsed her own reflection cast back by the tinted window, streaked with flashes of blue and red. The air was warm, the breeze cool against her cheek. She said, slowly, "He would have threatened me with that..."

"What?"

"When he broke. When he lost his temper and screamed... he would have threatened me with what he did to the other victims. He wanted to horrify, to shock me, yes? To scare me? He would have said what he did to them. But he didn't."

"I'm not tracking, Ilse."

"It's... it's not a evidence trail, Tom. I'm just telling you, if he'd really commited the murders we're talking about, he would have threatened me with what he did to them. He hunts in the woods. Not in a public shopping center."

"He doesn't have an alibi, Ilse. He works in the *woods.* Just like you said."

Ilse shifted on her foot, no longer looking in the direction of the sedan. She could feel her breath coming in short puffs, and she consciously paused, focusing and trying to inhale more deeply. She knew she was right... At least, she felt strongly she was.

The predator in the back seat wasn't the same one who'd killed the others. Wasn't the same one to wheel incapacitated women around in public.

Then again, Sawyer made a point. No alibi. Admitting to a murder. Clear connection to the most recent victim. An MO that matched...

Mr. Toman was an evil man.

But Ilse wasn't certain he was their evil man.

"I... maybe you're right," Ilse said. "Either way, we're arresting him. He's going to spend the rest of his life in prison, most likely. So... it can't hurt if I double check something."

"Double check what, exactly?"

"I..." she bit her lip. "I think I need to make a call."

CHAPTER TWENTY TWO

Sophie smiled across the hood of the car, beaming towards where Marquee was setting out their picnic. The sun was beginning to dip on the horizon, falling over the skyline, and slipping behind the mountains. She watched as the final rays tinged the clouds in vibrant colors.

Sophie couldn't shake how lucky she was.

"It's beautiful," she said simply.

Marquee looked up, his green eyes flashing, his perfect bronze skin like something out of a summer advertisement. She'd often thought her new husband should have gone into modelling.

Behind them, from the speakers of the car, a faint crooning voice carried over the cliff.

Sophie's feet dangled over the edge, her toes pointing towards the small lake at the bottom of the drop off. Trees around them, moss pattering the ground, the faint scent of mushrooms lingering on the air, tinging the breeze in something earthy and warm.

She kicked her feet, watching the way her toes swished over the waters below. The sound of a small, tumbling waterfall only added to the faint hum of music. She couldn't see the waterfall from where she sat, but she remembered it from yesterday's hike, when they'd decided to come back to the cliff for an evening picnic.

Marquee flashed his million dollar smile, his perfect teeth set. He winked at her. "You look hot," he said.

She snorted. "Nice one."

He shook his head. "Hey, I'm not the one studying to be a writer. Mechanics are allowed to say, *hot.*"

She winked. "I'll take what I can get." She watched as her husband set plastic forks next to the paper plates. He'd been in charge of food for today, so she wasn't very surprised when she spotted tubs of potato salad and cold, gas-station sandwiches. But she didn't mind. She wasn't here for the food anyway.

She glanced down at the ring around her finger. It was the prettiest ring any of her friends had seen. Two loops of diamonds wrapping in a twisting, vine pattern. Marquee had saved months to afford it. She had it on good authority, the reason he'd sold his newer car and bought a cheaper one, was so he could go the proverbial extra mile.

She felt like the luckiest woman in the world.

"I wish honeymoons didn't have to ever end," she said quietly, allowing her voice to mingle with the music from the car.

"Why should it?" her husband said, grinning. "Honeymoons are a mindset."

She chuckled. "I wish. I guess paying bills is a mindset too."

"Exactly. Here, do you want mustard potato or mayo radish?"

She wrinkled her nose, her feet grazing the boulder beneath her as she shifted on her hands, feeling the faint prickle of pine needles beneath her fingers. "I'm not even sure what that—umm, hello? Sorry, are we on private property?"

Her husband turned as well, frowning in the direction of the man moving towards them.

He didn't pause, didn't say anything. He just kept coming, moving through the trees.

"Hello?" Marquee said, pushing to his feet now. "Hey—sorry, man. We were told this was public property. Is the music bothering you? Sorry. I can turn it down."

The man didn't say a word. Didn't speak. He just kept coming towards them. He wore a hood, raised up, his eyes fixated on the two of them, though. His gaze, however, kept darting towards Sophie. His eyes flashed beneath that hood, and she felt a faint shiver up her back.

"Marq," she whispered. "Let's go. Please, no—forget the salad. Let's go."

Her husband wasn't the type to back down from anything. But at her insistence, he reluctantly grabbed his keys from where he'd rested them on the blanket. He tried to start folding the picnic set up, but now, the man striding towards them had broken into a jog. He was only twenty paces away. Fifteen.

Closer... closer...

"Marq, get in the car!" she barked. "Please. Forget the blanket. Go—go!"

The man still wasn't speaking as he jogged towards them. He wasn't sprinting. Wasn't speaking. Just encroaching with the inevitability of a sunrise.

Now, Sophie scrambled off the stone bluff, grabbed her husband's hand and pulled him towards the vehicle. The doors, fortunately, were still open. As the two of them tumbled into the front seats, the doors slammed, and Marquee locked his.

The man in the hood was now at their picnic site, approaching the car. Still quiet as a grave.

"Go!" Sophie yelled. She couldn't say where the sudden bout of terror was coming from except the certainty that this person intended to harm them. "Go! Go!"

Her husband, who worked as a mechanic, slipped the keys into the ignition with practiced experience. He twisted them, the engine turned and the brake lights flashed across the scattered pine needles. The headlights illuminated the drop off, the lake below. But the beauty was tainted now.

Fingers knocked against the window, but Marq wasn't paying attention. He yelled, through the window, "Get out of the way!"

"Roll the window up!" Sophie yelled suddenly. The back window was still cracked where they'd opened it to allow a breeze the night before.

And suddenly, a gloved hand shot through the window.

"Marq!" she screamed. "He's going for the lock!"

Her husband double checked the doors were locked. Cursing now, he began backing away, shredding through pine needles, kicking up leaves.

The man couldn't reach the lock, thank God. But suddenly, she heard a faint *hissing* sound. He was holding something in his hand, pointing it into the car. It sounded like hairspray.

But then, Marq surged past the hooded figure. The gloved hand, and whatever it had been holding, yanked out of the window.

The car sped backwards, spinning onto the road. The window rolled up completely now as Marq fiddled with the buttons while simultaneously speeding away.

Sophie let out a faint sigh of relief as they rerighted and began picking up pace, hastening away on the dusty road. She checked her pocket and felt another flash of relief at the outline of her phone. She'd been worried she'd left it behind.

Now, all that weird creep had was the potato salad and picnic blanket.

She hoped he choked on it.

"Holy crap," Marquee was saying as he floored the gas. In the rearview mirror, Sophie spotted the dark silhouette standing by the picnic site, watching them leave.

"That was close?" her husband said, laughing suddenly. He slapped a hand against the wheel. “Very damn close. Wow. I can’t wait to tell the guys back... back at...” He blinked now, wrinkling his nose and inhaling slower. “Tell... I...” His voice was now mumbling. The car slowing.

“Marq?” she said, panicked.

But then she felt it too. There, all the windows closed, she thought she detected the faintest scent of *something* lingering on the air. But as she breathed, panicked, in-out, desperate gulps. Her fear increased. She wanted to say something, but her mind was confused now.

She tried to speak, but her words came slurred.

It barely registered now as Marq drove off the road. Slower... slower.

They bumped into a tree. The front tires dipped into a ditch.

The brake lights illuminated a faint, grassy slope behind them. Sophie tried to speak again, but she felt... what was happening... how...

She couldn’t even process her thoughts.

And then, in the rearview mirror, she spotted a figure slowly moving towards them.

As if he had all the time in the world.

A man in a hood was approaching their car. His feet took the slanted incline, trampling through the grass. The faint red glow of the brake lights illuminated his form as he stepped towards them, in slow, cocksure motions.

No sound from him. He didn’t speak.

Neither could Sophie now. She wanted to scream. Wanted to...

Black spots danced across her vision. Her husband’s head was now leaning forward, bumped against the steering wheel.

She tried to wake up, but couldn’t even move. Her eyes slipped as if her own neck had failed to support her head.

The last sight was of that beautiful, twisting diamond ring on her finger.

And then everything went dark.

CHAPTER TWENTY THREE

Ilse stood in the parking lot of the precinct, her phone pressed against her cheek, the smooth glass cold against her skin. She watched as Sawyer led Toman up the marble steps, accompanied by at least four other police officers. All pretense had vanished from their suspect. The admitted murderer was thrashing, trying to rip his arms free from where the officers guided him forward.

Evening had now approached, coming quickly, following the return trip from the forest preserve.

More than one call had come in on her phone from Agent Rawley, but Sawyer had forbidden her from answering.

It didn't feel right but in the end, she was going to let Tom take the lead. For the moment, she had her own phone calls to make.

As confident as Sawyer was that they had the killer...

It didn't match. Toman was a coward, a creep, and a predator who preferred privacy for his perversion. The killer they were hunting preferred public displays. He hunted women on closed sets, pushed them in front of trains. Or off parking structures in a busy mall.

The issue, of course, wasn't a matter of physical evidence. The killer had been careful in this regard. None of the victims showed trace DNA. The murder weapons had been gravity and a rope and a train. The killer was careful. Cautious.

Ilse shifted on the concrete, her arm brushing against the jutting mirror of the police cruiser at her side.

Finally, her phone connected.

"Hello? Ilse?" said the voice. "Becks? Is that you?"

She hid a smile at the familiar nickname. No matter how often she insisted her old mentor not use that name, he never seemed able to resist. She cleared her throat, and in her mind's eye, she pictured a smiling face, a Santa Claus beard, eyes that were always full of mirth. She pictured his prosthetic arm, and his favorite bicycle which he took everywhere. Ever since moving from her Lakeside home, it had been difficult to meet up with her old professor and her own counselor. It had been a while since she had seen him for a session, too. Months, in fact.

And now, listening to his voice over the speakers, she was equally filled with a sudden surge of joy and warmth, while doubling down on her hatred of all things technology. Something about speaking to Donovan Mitchell over a phone just didn't feel right.

"Dr. Mitchell," she said, trying to keep her tone cheerful despite the gloomy atmosphere of the police precinct. She leaned against the vehicle now, crossing her arms, and smiling off across the street.

Her eyes traced a small bakery with patio seating, the faint scent of freshly baked dough wafting on the air. She supposed, the police precinct offered free security.

"How's it going, Ilse?" said the cheerful voice. "You caught me at the perfect time. I was just about to head out for a ride with some of my friends—how can I help you?"

"Oh, sorry. Do I need to call back later?"

"No, of course not. I have time for you. How can I help?"

This final query cut. *How can I help?* As if he knew she were calling for something he could give her rather than out of any sense of fondness. Not that she could blame him. She didn't do a good job of keeping in touch with people. She would have to remember, in the future, to call him simply to say hi.

Now, with a faint prickle of guilt, she said, "I had a couple of questions. I'm working a case. I don't mean to intrude, so if you really do need to go, I'm perfectly fine–"

"It's fine, Ilse. I always have time for you. Shoot."

She shifted, smiling at the tone. But as her mind moved back to the business at hand, her smile vanished. "I'm having something of a disagreement with my partner on the psychological makeup of one of our killers. I don't mean to bother you, but...some of the details aren't pleasant."

"I've been watching the news," he said. "It makes me proud to see how far you've come, Ilse. It's about that guy who's been killing women in wheelchairs?"

"Yes, sir. I'm afraid it's worse than that. He's drugging them. Using some sort of anesthesia to keep them from moving while he wheels them about in public. Two of them he pushed off of structures. A parking lot, and a bridge. One he hung. Another he pushed in front of a train."

"Dear God," Mitchell said. "Did you catch him?"

"That's just it. We found a park ranger who fit the bill. He admitted to a murder, but not these murders. He does, however, have history with at least one of the victims. And has a pending trial for attempting to tranquilize a woman on a date."

So the physical evidence matches."

"Exactly."

"So what's the problem?"

Ilse bit her lip, considering how best to approach this. She wanted to present her thoughts as succinctly as possible. In the end, she said, "When I was tracking him in the woods, he was confident. The moment he was taken in front of police, he started acting like a little child."

"Typical behavior. Projecting his own insecurities. There's a colloquial term he might react to, actually. I heard about it on the Internet. Involuntary celibate."

Ilse shook her head. "Something like that."

"And so you don't think the man you have is the one guilty of the crimes?"

"I'm having a hard time making a connection. I don't know what comes next. All the physical evidence, the circumstantial evidence, suggests that we have our guy. But he doesn't match, and he didn't recognize the names of two of the victims."

"I wish I could be of more help. But you mentioned he was a ranger. Don't they sometimes carry tranquilizers?"

"Yes. But, the killer isn't using tranquilizers. According to one of the coroners, he's using a sort of general anesthesia. To confirm, I contacted another coroner and asked them to go over the toxicology report."

"And?"

"They haven't gotten back to me yet."

"Well, Ilse, you're not going to like it, but... do you remember what I used to tell you in our sessions?"

"Yes. *Pay the bill on time*."

Dr. Mitchell laughed, fading into a chuckle. "Funny. If I remember correctly, you forgot to pay half your bills. No, what I mean is that you have good instincts. I don't say it to everyone, but in your case, trust your instincts. And," he said, hesitantly, "how you're describing it suggests to me that there is more at play than simple narcissism."

"What do you mean?"

"Why parade them?"

"As displays. Trophies?"

"Perhaps. Or humiliation."

Ilse frowned, considering this. "Of course, that has to be part of it.

But what's your point?"

"Why humiliate them? Why isn't it enough for this killer of yours to murder and abuse, without risking himself. Unless, the death alone is not what he's after"

"You think maybe wheeling them around is the point."

"Perhaps even more than the murders themselves, yes. It's certainly possible. In my experience, and take this with a grain of salt, but people are most envious of what they once had."

"Say that again?"

"People most desire what they once had, but lost. Envy can take the form of desiring something you've never had. I admit that. But it is often strongest in longing after something you did have and lost. Does that make sense? If he is humiliating them, out of a place of punishing them, then it would seem they have something that he doesn't"

"Beauty? Jobs? Femininity?"

"I can't answer that part for you."

Ilse chuckled nervously. They both knew she was crossing some confidentiality boundaries by making this phone call to begin with. But Sawyer had started it by blocking Agent Rawley's number. She was trying her best. She frowned, considering it and thinking back to all the witness testimony. She considered the first victim, the hairdresser. A very talkative, gregarious woman. She thought about Riley Sanderson, a soccer player. The star on the team. Then she thought about the fashion model. The door-to-door salesman. What was one thing they all had in common?

Three were attractive, but one wasn't. Two were physically impressive...

Why was the killer drugging them? Wheeling them around.

No one saw him. Well, that wasn't completely true. They saw, but didn't notice.

Seen not heard.

She considered this for a moment. *Seen not heard.* An expression she had often used applied to children.

What someone had, but then lost.

Lopez was known for her ad with fireworks. A vibrant, ostentatious display. Riley Sanderson was known for scoring goals, celebrating those victories. The hairdresser was a talkative, energetic woman. So how did the door-to-door salesman fit?

She was someone who *talked* for a living. That was it, wasn't it?

"Dr. Mitchell, I think you're a genius," she murmurred.

“Undoubtedly, but I can’t take credit for whatever you’re thinking. Hopefully I helped. Now, look, I actually do have to go. I’m starting to get angry looks. Anyway, if ever you’re back in town, please don’t hesitate to stop by.”

Ilse bid her farewell, thinking hard.

What if...what the killer most envied was making noise?

That would explain how the door-to-door salesman fit with the others. Some of them were athletic, but not all. Some of them were beautiful, but similarly, there were exceptions. Some of them were successful in their careers, but again, stereotypically, a hairdresser or a salesman or even a high school student weren’t seen in this regard.

But outgoing, talkative, loud

It made sense. Didn’t it?

Maybe that was who he was targeting. So he was envious of people who made noise, who had the energy to talk and to greet strangers. Did that mean he was an introvert?

But she thought back to what Mitchell said. Something that he’d once had, but lost.

No, not introversion. Not a personality quirk. Medical. Something not just lost, but taken. What if the killer couldn’t speak?

Everyone who saw him mentioned his movement, mentioned how unnoticeable he was. Not a single one of them said he spoke a word...

Her phone began to ring.

Ilse jolted, glancing down, and briefly hoping it wasn’t Rawley again.

But no... an unfamiliar number.

She frowned, raising the phone.

“Hello, Dr. Beck.”

“Hello? This is Dr. Anderson.”

“I’m sorry, do I know you?”

“Yes, this number requested a toxicology report on the recent murders of Tiffany Perkins, Erin Pratt, and–”

“Yes,” Ilse said excitedly. “That’s right! I was trying to get a second opinion. What did you find?”

“The same thing the first coroner did. “It’s an anesthesia. However, it is not one used commonly in human surgeries.”

Ilse frowned. “Excuse me?”

“Dr. Jordan, who I know and respect, made a small mistake. The anesthesia is not found in hospitals. It’s found in animal clinics. Veterinarians.”

"Are you sure?"

"Very. He was right, however, that it is being altered somehow. I can give more details. But essentially what he said was accurate. The only small adjustment I would make is that this type of anesthesia is used in animal surgeries, not human. Hopefully that helps."

"It does. It helps a lot. Thank you. You don't happen to know who distributes that paralytic, do you?"

"I do, in fact. It's pretty common, but that information is far easier to access than hospital records. I can give you the name; you should be able to call the manufacturer."

"Perfect. I'm ready—what's the name?"

CHAPTER TWENTY FOUR

Why hadn't she come home yet?

He sent postcards and she didn't care. He came to visit, and she wasn't there. It was enough to make a man crazy.

He flung a small plate across the room. Small bits of granola scattered where the porcelain shattered against the wall.

He inhaled slowly, pacing, feeling his rage simmering. He glanced towards the door, his sleepless, bleary eyes fixating on the frame. Did she know?

Was she playing him? Right now, were FBI agents camped outside the complex?

He sprinted towards the window, pushed the blinds aside and peered into the street.

No FBI. No sign of any threat.

"Where are you, Hilda?" He murmured beneath his breath.

He glanced down, staring at a few shards of the plate he had smashed. Then he looked at his hand, staring towards where he gripped the small, steel scaling knife. He'd been practicing. Buying different cuts of meat from the store, just to perfect his technique. He had even decided what pattern to inflict.

He exhaled slowly.

He had to be patient. She was FBI. In the past, she had spent nights in hotels, hadn't she?

Patient. Yes, that was it. He had to be patient.

And yet even as he thought it, trying to calm himself, he could feel his temper threatening to boil over.

He had come this far, though. He couldn't let a little temper tantrum ruin everything. This was Hilda Mueller's surprise party.

A horrible little thought crossed his mind. What if she was flying to Germany?

He began scratching at his arm with the knife, shifting uncomfortably and shaking his head.

"No, no," he muttered to himself. "No, she's coming. She *is*."

He was rocking on his heels now, wincing and muttering and pacing again.

An incessant ritual. He moved away from the window; he didn't want to be seen.

He had time. Already, he had been waiting in her apartment for hours. Through the night. She must've stayed at a hotel. That was the only explanation.

Maybe, if she had spent the night in a *different* bed, he should return the favor in hers.

He had already gone through her clothing drawers. There were some very interesting items, and now, he would sleep on her bed. Maybe use her shower.

The thought made him smile. There were so many things he could do while waiting. Try her food. Look on her computer. This was a treasure trove of information.

"This isn't a drawback, it's a gift," he said, speaking to convince himself.

He had to think like this. A gift. Not a drawback. A boon. And in the meantime, even if she was in Germany, she would eventually return. Her stuff was still here. Yes. Sooner or later, he would get his shot. In fact, the more time he spent here, the more fun he could have. Waiting, anticipating, practicing.

Would he do it in the kitchen? Blood stained upholstery. The bathtub?

He clicked his tongue, his mood improving dramatically as he thought of all the ways he would take out even this frustration on Hilda Mueller. She would return eventually. And when she did, he would be waiting.

CHAPTER TWENTY FIVE

Ilse sat back in the break room of the precinct. Now, Sawyer was with her. He stared across the table, tapping a finger against the wooden surface. Ilse similarly fidgeted, waiting for the phone to connect. To his credit, Sawyer had taken a break from processing their new suspect in order to help her with her lead.

Ilse hadn't intended to distract, but at this point, Tom trusted her...

"Just those seven?" Ilse said, trying to keep the anticipation from her tone.

Sawyer, on the other hand, was also talking, but he looked uncomfortable. The reason was apparent, as he said, "I know it is somewhat irregular. But I need to know. Yes, employees. Anyone who works at your office, especially if they have access to anesthesia or the surgical unit."

Ilse waited, listening to the response on her own end. She sighed. "Alright, just those seven. The ones you sent me? Thank you."

She hung up.

Sawyer was saying, "I told you, I can't be specific. We're looking for anyone with a speech impediment or a difficulty hearing."

Ilse and Sawyer both waited, listening for the response. Ilse could hear the faint buzz of the voice over the speaker.

She watched her partner, feeling a slow jolt of excitement as Tom turned his attention to the yellow legal pad on the table and began hastily jotting information down.

"Alright, and how do I spell that?" Sawyer waited, and then said, "thank you for your time." He hung up.

"So it was only those seven?" He said, looking at her now.

Ilse nodded. "Did you get a chance to call all of them?"

Sawyer tapped his pen against the yellow legal pad. "Mhmm. We're sure there are no more vets in the area?"

"None that use this particular anesthesia," Ilse said.

"And how confident are we on that side of things? If Dr. Jordan could miss so horribly..."

Ilse frowned. Sawyer kept emphasizing this part. That Dr. Jordan was the one who had made the mistake.

“I mean, he’s probably not very good at his job,” Sawyer was saying, shaking his head in mock sympathy.

Ilse bit her lip, deciding not to comment.

Sawyer said, “So here’s what I’ve got. One person who is deaf. A woman.”

Ilse shook her head. “Everyone agreed they saw a man.”

Sawyer nodded, and crossed the name off his legal pad.

“The next has a speech impediment but he’s out of town for a conference.”

“Maybe we can put an asterisk next to his name?”

“No point, I already checked with the airline. He’s in New Jersey. Has been for a week.”

“Anyone else?”

Sawyer tapped his pen against the paper again. He nodded, shifting in the chair, and rocking back on the wooden furniture piece. The chair creaked beneath him as he shifted his weight.

“A man who is mute, and another man who is deaf. They both work at different clinics.”

“Do both of them have access to the same anesthesia?”

Sawyer nodded.

She winced. “Do we have anything else on them?”

“Neither of them are veterinarians. But they do assist.”

Ilse shook her head. She glanced at Sawyer, and added, “Thank you for helping.”

He shrugged. “Some of us are good at our jobs, unlike Dr. Jordan.”

“I get it.”

Sawyer smirked.

Ilse slowly pushed from the table, shaking her head. “I guess we should check each one. There’s two different addresses.”

“The last time we split up,” Sawyer said, “you almost got attacked.”

Ilse tapped her holster on her hip. “I was fine. It will be fine. Which one do you want?”

And again, she was reminded of dividing at the forest preserve. Sawyer taking the high route, moving up the incline. Ilse walking towards the lake.

It felt the same, and yet, somehow, though they were just talking about names and addresses, she couldn’t help but shake a slow, cold sense of impending doom. If they were wrong, and if she was right. And if the killer was really out there, then time was running out.

***

Ilse tested the speed limit of the borrowed sedan. The siren wailed above. She had decided to keep it going as long as she drove along the highway, only turning it off once she reached the subdivision.

She glanced at the GPS, which was leading her to the man who couldn't speak. There was scant information about him online, or in the database. The drivers license photo was from seven years ago. The license had expired. The man had a mullet, and dark eyes. He was frowning in his photograph. Besides this, the only information she had was of a civil lawsuit the man had filed against a hospital. This, however, was proving more difficult than she had anticipated to access. For some reason, the information from the hospital's legal case was hidden. Hiding behind red tape, most likely. Hospitals often found legal loopholes in her experience.

Sawyer was heading to the other house. In fact, as she glanced at the clock on her dashboard, he had likely already arrived.

The siren wailed, vehicles pulling aside to allow her passage. Now, evening stretched. Night would soon fall. Ilse felt a slow, creeping sense of horror. If she didn't reach the killer in time, there was no telling how many bodies he would leave today. Yesterday, he had killed three.

She picked up the pace, and only as she followed the GPS onto an off ramp did she finally turn the siren off. She didn't want him to hear her coming.

Suddenly, her phone rang.

Eyes on the road, one hand gripping the steering wheel, her foot aching from the constant changes in speed, she reached out, snagged the phone from the chair next to her, and answered. "Tom?"

"Ilse? I'm here. At the second guy's house. He's home with his wife. It's not him. Nice couple, but I'll keep a police presence by just in case..."

"You're sure?"

"Pretty sure. The guy is a bit *larger* than anyone the witnesses described."

Ilse let out a hissing puff of air. "Alright, thanks. And Tom, you might want to–"

"I'm headed your way. Just stand by. Wait till I get there."

Ilse gave a noncommittal grunt. She hung up. She had already called back up to meet her. But she was ahead by a few minutes. Every second that passed was another life risked. She couldn't sit idly by. She had to do something.

And so Ilse continued to follow the GPS. She took the turn onto the house's street, eyes darting along the structures lining the road.

Suddenly, the GPS chirped, *arriving at destination on right.*

Her heart skipped a beat, her eyes darted to the small, white letters on a mailbox.

This was it. The address of the man who worked for the clinic. A mute. In a way, she supposed it made sense.

But she was determined not to get ahead of herself.

She pushed out of the vehicle, hastening towards the front door.

No lights.

No sight of a car in the driveway or garage.

She knocked on the door, her heart pounding.

No response.

She felt a flicker of frustration and knocked louder, pressing the doorbell.

Still no response.

Lights were off. She couldn't see any movement through the window.

To the side, though, she spotted a fluttering curtain.

She stepped forward, frowning and pressing her cheek against the glass. Through a gap in the curtain, she spotted pictures.

They were difficult to make out at first, so she pulled her small, dumb phone from her pocket.

Then, realizing the flashlight would just reflect off the glass, she bit her lip.

Sawyer wasn't there with her. Normally, she could count on him to find a shortcut.

But now, it was up to her. Should she wait? She thought she heard sirens behind her, approaching from the main avenue.

Now or never. If she wanted a look, she needed to–

—a small shattering sound. Her elbow found the window.

And then, her flashlight clicked on. Without the glass, the reflection didn't obscure her vision. She shone the light into the house, illuminating the back wall.

And her heart nearly stopped. Adorning the wall, pushed with safety pins into brown cork, there were pictures of the victims.

All of them. She recognized Tiffany Perkins. Erin Pratt. Riley Sanderson. Regina Lopez. And there, another face. But this last one she didn't recognize. A young woman. Smiling, and it looked as if the photo had been cropped. In the image, the woman was holding up her hand, displaying a wedding ring.

Ilse stared, frozen. The small flash of light from her dumb phone spotlighting the horrible images.

Each of the victims had a large red X-mark crossing their lips.

He had silenced them. The last image of the woman with the wedding ring, though, displayed no such mark.

Ilse felt a flicker of horror.

And then hastily she withdrew her phone and immediately dialed Sawyer.

She waited, her foot tapping against the ground. She no longer felt guilty about shattering the window.

He answered. "Are you okay?"

"Fine. It's him. Tom, it's him."

"What was the name again?"

"Brian Ortega."

Sawyer mumbled something, then refocused, "Alright, I'm almost there."

"He isn't here. I think he's looking for someone else. A woman, a young woman with a wedding ring."

"I need more than that. What woman?"

Ilse felt a flash of frustration. The image had been blown up, zoomed in. She didn't have a clue who he was going after.

"His phone number," she said quickly. "We can track it, right?"

"Depends on a couple of things. But theoretically."

"Good. Do that. Tell me where he is! I have a horrible feeling..."

CHAPTER TWENTY SIX

Ilse raced up the cliff, tires squealing and kicking dust in spurts. She heard the swish of the waterfall, the tumbling pulse of liquid hitting the surface of the small lake. The sun had fallen. Now, night stretched its dark fingers across the horizon. The moon watched. Ilse listened as Sawyer guided her over the phone, leading her up the cliff. She could hear him cursing, the sound of honking horns as he hastened in her direction. But he was more than ten minutes away.

"Take it slow," Sawyer was saying, "it might already be too late."

"I get it. Just tell me where to turn."

"It's coming up. Wait, all right, see a barn ahead?"

"There's no damn barn," she shouted into her speaker. She glanced through the windshield, her eyes moving across the trees.

She didn't know where to look. Thick trunks, obscuring leaves, swishing branches hid the roadside.

There was no barn. No structures at all. Just more forest. More–

There.

"I see it? Is it large and green?"

"I can't tell from the GPS pictures. That's probably it. You should be looking for an outcrop. There's a lover's bluff."

"A what?"

"Look for a cliff over the waterfall. It's some romantic spot."

"His GPS is on this cliff?"

Sawyer cleared his throat uncomfortably. "We lost the signal three minutes ago. I didn't want to alarm you."

Ilse yelled. She veered up the cliff, still kicking up dust. "What do you mean you lost the signal?"

"I'm sorry. I don't know. He must've turned his phone off or something. Maybe he got what he came here for."

"Why didn't you tell me?"

"Where else is a newly married young woman going? She's there. Trust me."

Ilse hissed in frustration as she threw the car in park, then shoved out of the front seat. Her phone was glued to the side of her face.

"Alright, I'm here. Can you see where I am?"

"No. We weren't tracking you. This takes time, Ilse. Just head up that road. There's a fork, take the left side. You'll be near the cliff, facing the waterfall in no time. I'm almost there. Be careful. Wait for me if you think–"

Ilse hung up. She didn't need the voice over the phone to alert the killer. Besides, there was no way she could wait. Not knowing that the killer was likely already out there. He was already on the move.

She broke into a sprint, racing up the incline, feet slapping against the unpaved ground. The trees shook and shivered above her.

Again, she was reminded of how much she hated walking through the woods on her own.

She hastened towards the top of the hill, her heart pounding wildly.

The dark tree branches extended towards her like spindly fingers, grasping at her silhouette. The wind howled, tossing her hair and tugging at her clothing. The waterfall tumbled over the cliff, crashing into the lake below—she could just glimpse the spray, speckling dark stone.

Ilse swallowed, picking up the pace still until she was now racing beneath the trees, towards the lookout spot Sawyer had mentioned. How had they lost the signal?

Had he been expecting them?

She could feel her stomach twisting, threatening to drop into her toes.

She paused, one foot resting on a wooden stair built into the side of the hill.

Breathing heavily, she glanced over her shoulder, back down the incline, towards were she had parked haphazardly.

No other vehicle in the parking lot.

Was she in the wrong location?

Then again, Ortega's license was expired. Maybe he didn't drive.

But what about the victims?

If someone had been determined, they would have been able to drive their car up the incline. In fact, if she looked in the dust, she thought she saw signs of tire tread. But she wasn't a woodsman like Sawyer. Her partner was still en route. For now, she was on her own, and she had to make a decision.

In three days, she was supposed to get on a plane and help put Gerald Mueller back behind bars. The BKA team she coordinated with did not see things the same way as the parole board had. Everyone knew Gerald was a threat, and if she didn't show up, that would mean he would escape again...

Exhaustion weighed heavy on her. Part of her wanted to retreat back to her car and wait for backup. And yet, his phone had led them here. Now it was off. Something had changed in the last few minutes.

And when it came to killers, change was never a good thing. It meant desperation. It meant strategy. It meant many things.

And so, summoning her resolve, and moving beneath the bristling shadows of the canopy, Ilse picked up her pace. Faint flecks of chilled water dappled her skin, rising up in a mist over the edge of the rocky outcrop. Moss pattered the side of the gray stone. The vegetation left a faint fragrance on the air, and only added to her sense of isolation. This was not the realm of humans. This was the wilderness.

She remembered how much time she has spent in her lake house, sitting on her porch, peering through the glass at the trees in the water. It had all seems so beautiful at the time. But beauty observed was far better than racing through it at a dead sprint.

She took the wooden stairs, practically skipping to the top. Ahead, she spotted an overlook.

A figure was moving towards her along the path—a jogger, wearing bright orange wristbands. He was also pushing a large stroller in front of him with the shade down. He whistled as he moved towards her, and smiled, nodding once.

She ignored him, glancing one way, then the next. And suddenly, ahead, she spotted a car.

She broke into a sprint.

Six steps.

And then it hit her like a load of bricks. She spun on her heel, glancing back.

"Excuse me?" She called out.

He was still whistling.

"Excuse me, sir?" She said, louder.

He stopped now, and bent over to tie his shoe. He reached up a finger, adjusting an earbud.

She couldn't hear the music, but imagined it was loud enough to drown out her voice.

She frowned, torn, glancing towards the parked car, which looked as if it had driven off the road. Then her gaze switched back to the man with the stroller.

It was a very large stroller.

Ilse began to move, slowly. The man was still on one knee,

whistling, tying his shoe. She drew closer, closer. Hand on her holster. She slowly unclipped her weapon.

"Sir, I don't mean to alarm you, but I need you to turn slowly–"

There were no earbuds. He had heard her perfectly well but had been acting. And now, as she came to within a few feet, he spun, snarling, raising a small aerosol can, and pressed. A sudden jet of vapor shot into her face, and she felt a chill prickle along her skin.

She yelled, stumbling back, reaching for her weapon, trying to pull it.

Now, she spotted the two adults crammed into the baby stroller, beneath the small protective plastic cover.

A jumble of arms and legs, both motionless. No movement. Dead already?

As she pulled her gun, the killer spotted it, yelled, an incoherent, wordless cry, and surged in. His head collided with her chest. An explosion of pain. Dark spots across her eyes. She stumbled, gasping. Hit the ground, and let out a long groan.

She twisted, still groaning, and raised a hand. Her weapon was sent skittering, kicked by his boot.

And now, she detected a strange scent. Like nothing she had ever inhaled before. But as she tried to rise, struggling to push up, dark spots began to dance across her vision. And that's when she knew she was in trouble.

Her fingers were tingling. Her legs limp.

She could barely rise.

She spotted where the man was stooping to pick up a boulder. A small, thick rock about the size of her head.

As he grunted, trying to lift it, for intentions she could easily guess, he placed his aerosol can on the ground.

Desperate, her gun lost, she surged for the can.

He yelled, stomping. Missed.

He dropped the stone on her wrist. Something snapped.

She howled in pain, but even this sound came slurred. Her lips weren't working. Her vocal cords thick.

Like a drowning woman, lunging for the last glimpse of a lifeline, she snatched at the aerosol can, struggling to lift it.

Her fingers scrambled against the chill metal; she raised the thing and squeezed.

The killer had been lunging at her, yelling incoherently again. He didn't use words, just sounds.

And suddenly, as he reached for her, fingers outstretched, as she rolled on a dusty, pine needle strewn ground, another jet of vapor shot from the nozzle, hitting the killer in the face.

He roared in anger and tried to kick her in the head.

The blow hit her falling arm.

More black spots.

And now she could feel the strange paralytic having its way.

She couldn't move, her arms limp.

He tried to pick up the rock again. He managed to lift it to his knees, higher. But then his arm buckled.

He yelped. The stone fell, hitting Ilse on the same cracked wrist.

Whether from the pain, or the strange drug, Ilse succumbed.

The last image she glimpsed was of an irate, furious man, reaching towards her throat. Fingers around her neck, squeezing. No backup. Two bodies in the baby stroller. Most likely dead

She'd come too late. And now she was about to die as well.

The fingers tensed on her throat. But then, the grip loosened, almost imperceptibly.

But her vision was gone. Her consciousness followed.

CHAPTER TWENTY SEVEN

Ilse blinked, her eyes fluttering. The moon flickered above, like a hazy flashlight.

She groaned, and her mouth felt like cotton.

She pushed up, but then she yelled in pain. Her wrist was broken.

She tried to use her other arm. This, despite her best efforts, didn't work either. She let out a growl, as she pushed despite her injured arm, to her knees.

And there, she knelt in the dusty road, blinking and gasping, spittle down the side of her face. Hands caked in dust and mud.

She blinked, and realized somehow she had cut her forehead. Blood trickled down the corner of her eye, and then she heard moaning at her side.

The killer was lying on the ground as well. He was slower at first, but then he started to rise too. He rolled from his back onto his belly. He tried to push up, but his arms didn't have the strength yet.

Her panic flared.

Whichever of them got to their feet first would be able to go for her gun.

She could see it, in the middle of the road, a small black wedge against the ground. The shadows above attempted to hide the weapon. Now, she realized the killer was eyeing her gun as well.

In a strange, desperate, silent race, the two of them struggled to their feet.

Neither of them slowed. Both of them emitted strange, huffing sounds.

The wind continued to whistle. The figures in the stroller were motionless. Either they had gotten a larger dose of that strange drug, or they were already dead.

Ilse managed to reach her feet first.

As she stumbled towards her weapon, she paused long enough to kick the can of spray away from the killer, sending it clattering off a tree trunk and into the underbrush.

The killer tried to snatch at her ankle. His fingers missed, but snared her shoe. His pinky lodged between her laces, pulling.

She groaned, yanking her leg forward. She thought she heard something *snap*.

Both of them, injured, in agony, like some sort of audition for a zombie TV show, stumbled and groaned and moaned, struggling to reach the gun in the middle-of-the-road.

The killer had only managed to gain his knees, but he refused to let go of her shoe. Even with his broken finger, he held on. She tripped.

Hit the ground. Swallowed dust. Gasped.

He was crawling over her now, sending chills up her spine and body.

The touch was revolting. She tried to buck her hips. Managed to dislodge him.

He hit the ground again, with a yelp.

He tried to reach for her hair, his fingers scraping through as he attempted to grab hold.

Again, chills of revulsion accompanied his motions. She bit at his hand.

And like this, desperate, scrambling through the mud, the two of them reached the gun at the same time. One hand pulling, a foot kicking, teeth biting, fingers scratching. It was difficult to see where Ilse's attacks started, and where his did. The two of them were crawling over each other, both bloodied. Both broken. Both mewling, desperate, terrified.

She could smell the fear. It was partly her own, but also, in every motion, and every action, emanating from the horrible man crawling towards her weapon.

No hesitation, she grabbed the gun–

He kicked.

He had spun around, grabbing at her foot now, and twisting it.

She had taken jujitsu before. This was not an experienced practitioner. He was fighting desperate and feral, trying to reach for anything he could snap off.

His kick, however, sent the gun flying again.

Now his head faced her feet.

She tried to rise. He tripped her.

She spotted the gun land in the weeds by the edge of the cliff. The sound of the waterfall below continued to thrash.

She kicked out, catching him in the chin. He lost his grip. Picking up pace, feeling her nerves responding quicker, she scrambled towards her weapon.

He yelled, and surged after her. The two of them reached the clump of weeds at the same time.

Now, though, on the edge of the cliff, he didn't get too close. He eyed her, warily, blinking, and desperately searching the weeds, the grass for her gun.

In between glances in his direction, she also searched for the weapon.

There!

No, a pinecone. *Shit*.

He lunged, snatched something, but it was a branch. He flung it at her. Missed. The thing arced end over end, plummeting towards the waterfall below.

Ilse risked a quick glance. The tumbling liquid turned white where it hit the dark waters. Ripples spread out across the small lake. Thick, dark stones like teeth extended towards them, as if threatening any encroachment. Ilse and the killer both scrambled in the weeds on the edge of the cliff.

Each of them, desperately, playing the gamble that whoever found the weapon first would leave and whoever didn't, would likely end up at the bottom of the cliff.

Her fingers tore through thistle and briar. She found sticks, stone. Where was the damn gun?

He kept his distance still. Whether he had sensed she knew how to navigate a tussle, or if he was naturally cautious, he kept a few feet back, also looking for the weapon.

He seemed to have given up the search, though, and she spotted where he was now reaching for a large branch.

Images flashed of him striking her, sending her tumbling.

She couldn't let that happen. She tried to lunge in, but he darted back.

He hit her arm. The injured arm. She screamed in pain.

His eyes widened in excitement. Anticipation.

And then, a gunshot.

The branch in his hand exploded.

She heard a curse. Glanced back. Sawyer was taking aim. Lights flashed from the parking lot. She hadn't even seen him arrive.

Another police officer stood next to Sawyer, peering into the baby stroller while drawing his weapon as well.

Sawyer had been aiming too far to the left, and had hit the branch on a backswing. Most likely, he had been attempting to avoid her.

"Put your hands in the air!" Sawyer screamed.

But the killer wasn't listening.

"I said put them up!"

But again, Sawyer received no compliance. In fact, the louder he spoke, the more agitated the man became.

He thrashed at Ilse with his splintered branch, stabbing at her with the sharp end.

With one arm broken, it was a difficult move, but she had experience training to disarm. Experienced training with larger foes. She grabbed the branch, twisting. She pulled sharply, and he stumbled towards her. The palm of her hand left out, catching his chin.

He yelled. Hit the ground, hard. And suddenly she was on him. Knee to his chest, holding him down.

"Don't move," she said quietly. She used as few words as possible, trying to speak in nearly a whisper. If she was right, loud noises, too much speaking would only infuriate the man.

"Don't move," she repeated, as he was struggling.

Dark eyes stared up at her, glaring out from beneath a pronounced brow. He glared, but she met his gaze.

"Mr. Ortega," she said softly, "you're coming with us."

And suddenly he surged. One moment, she had her knee against him, his arm twisted. The next, with a scream of pain, he allowed her to break his wrist. And a knife appeared in his hand, pulled from his boot. He slashed at her neck, and Ilse remembered how Riley's boyfriend had been killed.

As she tried to stumbled back, she heard another gunshot.

This time, Sawyer hit, grazing the man's arm.

He spun like a top, yelled, and then went head over heels, tumbling off the edge of the cliff.

Ilse cursed, lunging forward, missing completely. Her arm was on fire.

And then, she watched, as Ortega hit the rocky teeth. He missed the lake completely. His body broke against stone.

She stared down, gaping at his broken form.

Sawyer was shouting behind her. She heard the sound of rapid footfalls.

And then, a shrill voice. "They're alive," the voice screamed. "Paramedics. Call paramedics!"

Sawyer reached her. The voice had been that of the officer with him. Sawyer was simultaneously calling in for more backup, while also gripping at her arm.

She winced, and pushed his hand away. "Broken," she managed to gasp out through gritted teeth.

He instantly let go. He stared at her. "Are you okay?"

"I think so. He hit me with something. A gas. It's in the trees."

And then, more dark spots. She felt lightheaded, and slowly lowered herself, using a tree trunk as something of a support, leaning back and dislodging pieces and strands of bark as she slid down and sat in a huddle at the base of the tree, her legs pulled up beneath her.

The pain in her arm was immense. The killer, gone. Vanished, like vapor. One moment standing before her, attempting to cause more ruin and misery.

The next, at the bottom of the cliff. Dead.

Gone.

Like that, it was all over.

"Did he say they were alive?"

"Looks like it. Look, doc, paramedics are coming. Just hang tight, okay?"

She nodded slowly. Her voice was still weak, trembling. "My arm hurts." She was pretty sure she had already told him this. And yet, lightheaded, it was difficult for her to speak, to think.

"Hang on," Sawyer said, his voice louder. "Dammit, Ilse, hang on. Keep your eyes open."

But it was just so difficult. Her eyelids drooped, closing slowly. And there, sitting on the outcrop, overlooking the lake, the dead killer, listening to the sound of police shouting at the base of the hill, she couldn't help but feel strangely tranquil. Not quite happy. Certainly in pain. But with Sawyer there, it felt as if she could be confident things were going to work out.

A strange assessment. But one she believed none the less.

More shouting Sawyer was now sprinting again, racing to fetch help.

Her head lowered, her eyes closed. She knew no more.

CHAPTER TWENTY EIGHT

The next afternoon, Ilse reclined in the hospital bed, wincing as Sawyer examined her cast with less than gentle probing fingers. "Do we get to sign it?" He said at last, lowering his hand.

She winced, shaking her head. "I'd be worried what you drew."

He grinned. "You did good, doc."

"Thank you. You too. You save my life. Again."

Sawyer shifted, a finger trailing against the armrest of the small, hospital bed. He shot a glance over his shoulder, watching as a nurse hastened past, moving in the other direction.

"Yeah, I think that just makes us even."

Ilse swallowed. She glanced down at her cast. Her arm still hurt. Thankfully, she had been given a couple of pain pills, though she had taken half dosage. She knew what those things could do if given too much influence.

"I don't think of it as a competition," she said quietly.

"What?"

"You said we're even. It isn't a competition. I would do it again. And I know you would do the same for me."

He shook his head, rubbing at his face. "See, that's why I like you, doc. You're a straight shooter."

"Same can't be said for you," she said, primly. "By my count, you missed twice."

Sawyer blinked. A second later, he realized she was joking. He shook his head ruefully. "That's not my fault. I was trying to avoid hitting you."

"Are you calling me fat?"

"Look at the jokes. Where is this coming from?"

Ilse shook her head. "Those painkillers are stronger than I thought."

Sawyer's mirth faded at this comment. He glanced at her injured hand, and shook his head. "I'm sorry about that. I wish I'd gotten to you in time.

"Don't worry about it. So is it true, what Rawley was yelling at you about?"

Sawyer glanced again through the open door. His eyes lingered on a small seating area, next to one of the nurse's desks. "Damn, you heard that?"

"I'm pretty sure the entire fourth floor heard that. I told you not to block the boss' calls.

"Rawley is harmless. His bark is way worse than his bite."

"At least he's happy we solved the case. If we hadn't, I'm not sure you'd still have a job."

Sawyer shrugged. "But yeah, what you asked—it's true."

"I didn't finish my question."

Sawyer's green eyes met hers. "You wanted to know if the killer was operated on at this hospital. Right?"

She blinked. This was, in fact, the part of the conversation she had been listening to. It hadn't taken much in the way of listening, as Rawley had practically been screaming at Sawyer. But something he had said stood out. The information request had come in on the civil suit she had found for Mr. Ortega. They had operated on his throat. A routine operation for a small polyp on his vocal cords. One of the doctors, at the time, had been drinking. His hands unsteady. According to the civil suit, he had severed Mr. Ortega's vocal chords. Had permanently destroyed the man's ability to speak.

Ilse felt a jolt of grief. It was all sad. That, she supposed, was what had set Mr. Ortega off. Dr. Mitchell had been right. People most envied the thing they once had.

And someone had taken Mr. Ortega's voice.

She sighed, shaking her head. "I hate that," she murmured.

"Which makes you good," Sawyer said. "If I'm honest, I don't give it a second thought. The idea of that guy suffering doesn't bother me at all. You're better than me. And I'm okay with it. But my offer still stands, by the way."

She blinked. "Oh, *that*?"

Sawyer just nodded. "It's just coffee. I'm not asking you to meet my parents."

The mere thought, even in jest, made her stomach flip. "That, if I'm honest, horrifies me."

"I figure. Don't worry, the old man is dead, and my mother won't like you regardless."

"Perfect. Tom, I don't, I don't want–"

"Why not?"

She blinked. Was this normally etiquette for turning down an offer to date?

She wasn't versed in the ritual, but she was pretty certain that people weren't supposed to question your choice. She thought of how much she enjoyed her time with Tom. How much he'd been able to bring her out of her shell. She never would have joined the FBI if not for Sawyer's encouragement. But more than that... he was a man who knew pain. Like her. But she couldn't bring him in... She never had. For nearly three decades, her life had been a one of secrets and pain. The mere thought of *sharing* that with someone else... She felt a tingle of horror. She closed her eyes briefly, feeling a jolt in her heart. Part of her wanted to blurt out a different answer. Wanted to... to... to what?

To admit feelings she kept hidden? To *have* feelings... Affection, fondness was beyond her control. She grit her teeth, forcing back the rising wave of tangled emotions.

"Because," she said, sighing in exasperation.

"That's not a reason. What is it? Do you think I'm ugly?"

She blinked, shook her head quickly.

"You think I'm hot?"

She snorted, her emotions sufficiently suppressed once again. "Are you sure you haven't been taking painkillers?"

He grinned, his green eyes sparkling. He adjusted the brim of his baseball cap and shrugged again. "Well, I guess I'm man enough to take no for an answer. All right, fair. I won't ask again. Unless you want me to."

"And how do you expect to determine that?"

"If you tell me. Or, you know, if I pick it up."

Ilse hesitated at this part. Sawyer had the emotional bandwidth of a tube of toothpaste. She wasn't sure she wanted to trust his intuition on whether or not he should broach the subject again. But she supposed, in that moment, she had escaped easy. No hurt feelings. And they could go back to being professional.

She shifted uncomfortably in the bed. Her eyes moved to the window, watching the sun. She had spent the night in the hospital, for observation. Technically, they wanted her to stay another few hours. But she was getting antsy. She had her wrist in a cast, was on painkillers, but otherwise she felt fine.

"What's going to happen to Sophie and Marq?" She said softly, using the first names of the married couple they had found jammed into the stroller.

"They're going to make a full recovery. It looks like he was going to take them to a second location. I don't want to think about what he had in store. You got there in time."

She felt a flicker of relief. She wanted to smile. But it was difficult. All she could think about where the other names.

So many dead. And yet, two would live.

She let out a faint sigh.

Sometimes, she wondered why she had gone into this line of work. She watched the sun. That question, she realized, only occurred to her during the daytime. At night, it was obvious. That's when things went bump in the dark.

She shifted, and, frowning, began to rise from her bed.

"Hey, they said you were supposed to stay put."

"Tom, answer seriously, when have you ever stayed as long as a doctor told you to?"

He paused, thinking, very hard. But then he shrugged. "Whatever. Need a ride?"

She hesitated, but then nodded. Things were back to normal, weren't they? He wouldn't bring up the subject of dating again. Maybe she should take a taxi. Just to be sure.

"It's no bother," he said, insistent. "Besides, taxis are expensive. Let me drive you."

She hesitated again, but then, as she pushed out of the bed, adjusting her sweater, she finally nodded.

Sawyer grinned. "Here, I'll grab your shoes."

CHAPTER TWENTY NINE

Ilse waved goodbye to Sawyer, flashing a quick, but uncomfortable smile where he idled in the car at the curb outside her apartment.

She shifted as she took the step leading to her front door.

The large apartment complex cast a shadow, but it wasn't an ominous one. More like shade in a desert. She just wanted to go home. To lay in bed, to inhale the fragrance of granola that she had left uncovered on the stove.

She imagined a warm bath, with bubbles and the faint crooning jazz played over the old radio she kept beneath her bed.

If she was lucky, there would still be some butter pecan ice cream in the freezer.

She shifted her arm, adjusting the sling which the doctor had insisted she wear. The cast scraped against the fabric of the sling.

She entered the code to her apartment and turned back, watching Agent Sawyer.

Tom gave another little wave.

He was hesitant, shifting uncomfortably in the front seat.

More than once, he glanced down, then up again, as if wanting to say something. He even rolled down the window, and she felt her heart leap. She wasn't sure she had the energy to deal with a conversation right now.

She had made the right decision, hadn't she? She shifted on the concrete step outside her apartment as the door buzzed and she pushed her fingers against the cold glass, leaving a smudge.

She paused, using the edge of her sleeve to wipe the fingerprints.

As she stepped into her apartment, though, she felt a flood of anxiety.

She winced, exited again, and allowed the door to close. She entered the number once more. Another buzz. She stepped in. And then she left. And like this, back and forth, she moved from inside the apartment onto the concrete step, and back. Four times.

And yet even after the fourth, she still felt a strange anxiety in her chest.

She shifted uncomfortably. Again, she glanced back in the direction of Sawyer.

He still waited by the curb. His hands gripped the steering wheel, and he stared through the glass. The window was still rolled down, as if at any moment he might call out.

She studied his silhouette. A strong jaw, and an ever present scowl as if the world at large had somehow offended him.

She watched Sawyer, but then...

...pushed back any sense of obligation.

She had turned him down. That was that. Simple enough.

She nodded to herself, and finally stepped through into the apartment, no longer looking back, and moving slowly to the stairs.

She took them one at a time, first one foot, then the next following onto the same stair. She felt very old all of a sudden. Like this, wincing, bruised, but still alive, she took the stairs back towards her own version of an oasis.

Thoughts of butter pecan ice cream had reached new heights. She decided that if there wasn't any left in the freezer, she would use one of those online grocery delivery sites. Then again... she often struggled to figure out even the most basic websites.

She paused outside her door, frowning at the carpet.

Slowly, she bent over, and picked up a small metal pin.

She stared at the thing.

The flickering, fading bulb in the ceiling had caught the pin, illuminating it.

She didn't recognize the item, though.

Frowning, pushing to her feet, she slipped the pin into her pocket, and then pulled her keys from the same pocket.

She slipped the keys into the lock, turning slowly, and pushed open the door to her apartment.

A faint scent of cinnamon. She smiled, inhaling.

Home sweet home. In a few days, she would be traveling to Germany. But she was determined, for the next seventy-two hours to do nothing but sleep and listen to music and bake food and play with bubbles.

She stepped into her apartment.

And that's when she saw it. Shattered fragments of porcelain amidst chunks of granola, all across her carpet.

She frowned, trying to make sense of the strange image. How had—

The door slammed. She heard the sound of feet. A shadow out of the corner of her eye. She tried to spin. Someone's hand was at her waist. She heard a shout. The gun in her holster—someone was grabbing it.

She spun around, elbow whirling.

Too late, fingers on her neck. Shoving. The gun was free.

She hadn't even been paying attention. The gun was on the hip with the broken arm in the sling. She hadn't had time to defend it.

She stumbled, her shoulder crashing into the wall. The door had slammed shut, and she heard the bolt. And then, gathering her senses, as terror flooded her, she stared.

A man was standing in front of her. Her own weapon in his hand. He had short, spiky gray hair. He wore an earring in one ear in the shape of a crimson skull. A small, ruby gemstone set in the earring.

His nostrils flared, as he inhaled deeply, panting, staring delightedly at her. His hand holding the gun was trembling so badly, she could practically hear it rattle.

"Wow," he was saying, "Wow, I can't believe it."

She stared, feeling prickles along her spine, her cheeks. She held out a trembling hand. "Hang on, you don't know who I am. This is a mistake. I'm an FBI–"

"Agent, yes. I know. It is such a pleasure to meet you in person." He was beaming now. His cheeks stretching like taffy. He revealed pale teeth, pristine, perfectly whitened, except for a single tooth. This one, to her astonishment, matched his earring. Ruby. As if he had a gemstone in his tooth.

He was shaking still, clearly excited.

The delight was palpable, and his obvious excitement sent more shivers along her spine.

"I have been waiting a very long time for this."

He knew she was an agent. Who was this? Why in the hell didn't she recognize him? Had she made a mistake? Was this the real killer?

"You don't remember me, do you?"

She shivered at the sudden look of hatred in his eyes. "I'm very sorry, but I interact with a lot of people. Please help me remember."

"You know what, I'm going to hurt you until you remember," he said, with a little squeak of excitement. He nodded to himself, wagging his head, his silver hair shifting. The many spikes from too much product were starting to leak, carried by sweat down his head in angry streaks.

Her back was to the wall, and she felt a gouge mark in the plaster.

Shards of a plate and bits of granola crunched beneath her foot as she took a shaky step backwards.

"Don't move," he snapped suddenly.

She went still.

He waved the gun away from the door. "To the bedroom. Now!"

She shook her head.

"I know how to use this. And I will. Trust me. Either you move away from that door, or I cover it with your brains."

She watched him, uncertain at first what to do. But then slowly, she began to shift away from the wall, her arm in pain from all the motion. She moved around the man, the ruby earring flashing as she stepped past him towards the hall.

He kept his distance, though, her own weapon clutched tightly.

"I've been waiting so long for this," he said, excited. "You won't believe how much I know about you, Hilda."

Ice down her spine. She whirled, staring.

He wagged his head in excitement.

"Hilda Mueller. Isn't that right? I know about your family. I know about Gerald, and his recent parole. I know about what happened in that basement."

He was speaking with more delight, more excitement. As he did, though, it was obvious he wanted to have an impact. He wanted his words to affect her. And yet, though she knew what he desperately desired, she couldn't deny him. She was stunned.

Not even Dr. Mitchell knew the extent of her past. Sawyer had no clue what her real name was.

And now, a stranger in her apartment, with a gun in her face was taunting her with information he shouldn't have.

"Who are you?" she demanded

But this question only further seemed to infuriate him.

"You don't know, do you? You're not pretending. You're really just that stupid." With that last word, he snarled, surged forward and shoved her. She yelled, and stumbled, hitting the floor.

A sudden jolt of pain. Her back twisted on impact against the ground. She felt something sharp against her elbow, and a faint trickle of blood. One of the shards of plate.

She tried to rise, but her arm was in too much pain. She couldn't move it.

Helplessly, on the ground, she stared up at the man with the gun.

"You have to help me remember," she said through pressed teeth, hissing through the pain. "I have clients, suspects, witnesses. Who are you?"

"We talked for like two hours," he screamed. "Two full hours. You were going to save me. You were *supposed* to save me. But you left me to die."

He was completely out of control. His eyes bugged, rage poured from him. His face turned red.

She didn't know what to say, didn't know how to appease the man.

"I still don't know what you're talking about. When did I not save you?"

"I came to you, nearly ten years ago. How can you forget. You nearly killed me!"

"How did I kill you?" She said, trying to keep her voice calm, and hoping, in doing so, that he would mirror the emotion.

At the same time, she struggled desperately to think back. Ten years? Ten years was a long time. How did she know him? She didn't recognize the voice. Certainly did not recognize his face. She would have remembered that red tooth. Would have remembered those bugging eyes.

His hand was still shaking where he gripped the gun. Was it an illness?

No. She realized, he was just excited, scared. This wasn't a common experience for him, she decided. He was not used to pointing weapons at people. She did, however, notice his other hand, fidgeting in his pocket. Every so often, she glimpsed the flash of a metal blade that he was pulling in and out, nervously fidgeting.

He had come armed. Had broken into her home, violating her oasis.

"You said I was too sick for you," he said, jutting his chin.

And suddenly, a faint echo of a memory.

She hesitated. "Wait, was this back when I was interning?"

"How the hell should I know? I was in pain. I wanted to die. You were my only hope, and you wanted nothing to do with me."

And suddenly, Ilse remembered.

A phone call. One of her very first. When she had been working for Dr. Mitchell, starting to build her own client list. She remembered the call, now. At the time, she had found it difficult to take male clients. Since then, she'd matured, and was able to handle men and women. But now, as she stared at the intruder, she vaguely remembered that voice. That same sense of urgency, of entitlement. That same deranged shift in volume.

“I don’t remember your name,” she said slowly, “but I think I remember the call. It was a consult. We were trying to find if we were a good fit.”

He scoffed, and stepped towards her as if wanting to kick at her. But, he paused, and snapped, “Of course,” he screamed. “Of course we were a good fit! You were the only one. The one who could’ve helped me. You were the only one. No one else understood. No one else did. I could tell, when I was talking to you. I could tell that you knew what it was like. Knew what it was to have a demon father. To have evil in your house. Knew what it was to be hurt. To barely survive.”

She listened, staring, still keeping her expression calm.

“I knew you were the one. How could you tell?” he said.

Deranged. He knew her name. Knew her background; he’d been studying her. “You’re the one who’s been sending those postcards,” she said slowly.

“And she wins the prize,” he crowed. “Of course, I’ve been the one. I was always the one. You were supposed to feel like I did. Chased to the very end of yourself. Suicidal. How the hell did you keep going? Why didn’t you just kill yourself? It would have made everything so much easier.” He was waving the gun around erratically. She propped up on her good elbow, trying to rise, slowly, so he wouldn’t lash out.

“But you know what, I’m glad you did. I *am* glad. I am glad that I now get to do this with you in person. Because, let me tell you something, you abandoned me to the wolves. I was in pain for seven years. I nearly killed myself four times. Look.” He was screaming. He ripped down his sleeve, and showed deep scars across his left wrist.

“You did this,” he screeched. “You did. And this is your mark too,” he yelled, pulling at his collar and revealing a scar around his neck in the shape of rope marks.

She just stared, stunned. In a strange, odd way, she almost felt a note of compassion, pity. How many clients had she worked with who were similarly in pain? How many times had she tried to help someone only to find out that things were scarcely improving. She remembered, years ago, when one of her clients took her own life. It had devastated Ilse.

She tried to think, but then realized the memory was somewhat foggy.

She vaguely seemed to remember passing the client on to Dr. Mitchell. It was a better fit; or at least she had thought at the time. She was only an intern, fresh out of school. She hadn’t been up to the task.

She still couldn't remember everything about the call, but, she remembered after the first ten minutes, she had tried to pass the buck. But then he had threatened to kill himself on the phone. He had said something similar: how they were meant to work together. How she was going to be his Savior.

And now there he stood.

Full of rage and contempt and self pity.

"I recommended your case to Dr. Mitchell. Didn't you ever go?"

"Don't blame *me*. You're the one who should've helped me. I didn't want Mitchell. He doesn't have a clue what it's really like. But you do. I know you do. I know about your father. I actually spoke with his girlfriend."

At this, she stared, stunned.

"Yes, see, now I can tell, you're scared, aren't you? I knew his girlfriend. She was the one, in fact, who told me about you. Said you would be a good fit. She helped me find out who you were."

Ilse remembered, her father's accomplice. His female partner who had lived upstairs. She had been the worst. Her father's rage, his abuse, was his fault but it never would have gone as far without his accomplice egging him on.

She still struggled to remember the face. Struggled to remember the woman.

"Oh, now I see it, the wheels are turning," he said, narrating with a cackle. "You think you're so smart. You thought you were too good for me. She said you would think that. Said you wouldn't take the case. She said that if I asked nicely, you might think about it. But I asked as nicely as I could, and you didn't care. And then my life was in danger."

"I seem to remember you threatened to kill yourself. When I asked you for your address to send help, you refused."

"That's not *help*," he said, spluttering. This time he did try and kick at her. A weak, pathetic effort, his foot barely grazing her knee.

"Help? They drag you off to a hospital, have someone sit watching you as if you're some prisoner. They then send you to some clinic, where they threaten you that if you don't go voluntarily, you know what they'll do? If you don't go voluntarily and sign their stupid papers, they threatened to keep you there on a judge's order. Threaten to ruin your life. That's what they do. And then they strip you naked, take pictures. It's humiliating, embarrassing. Subhuman."

As he spoke, he snarled, and he looked almost feral .

At the same time, she felt a flicker of sympathy. She knew what he was describing was true. She had had many clients in the past talk about how the system only seemed to serve to keep them away from society. It wasn't interested in helping. It was interested in protecting everyone else. Pain, trauma, so often, was seen as the victim's fault.

Now, she could see the result. A man who had refused help. Because a system had failed him. Because he'd experienced callous indifference in a bureaucratic solution. Not authentic compassion. Not genuine, long-suffering love.

There was no solution without real concern. Without true mercy. Without putting oneself in another's shoes.

She knew all of this. In fact, she wondered now, years later, if she might have taken the case.

This was the thin line. The one that divided those who hurt others, from those who sought help. A very thin line sometimes. She thought of her own life. Of her sister, Heidi. Both had grown up the same. They had ended up in very different places.

The thin line led to a road. And the roads diverged, heading in opposite directions.

And by the looks of things, this man, for the last ten years, had chosen a different path. One that ended with him in her apartment, clutching a weapon, and pointing it towards her.

"Why don't you put the gun down, and we can talk about it."

"No," he yelled. "Now get to your feet and go to the bedroom. I've already laid out the plastic sheet."

At this comment, she felt a faint shiver.

Her father's accomplice had been behind this. She had known that somehow, it would all come back to Gerald Mueller, and that small house in the woods by the lake.

And yet, she knew she needed to stall. She needed to find a way to get the upper hand. To get him to lower the weapon. It was the only way. But with a broken arm, she wasn't sure what good it would do.

"I don't believe you," she said, suddenly, her tone going cold. Compassion, gentle listening wasn't working. So she switched tactics. Aggressive. He might hurt her, but he would still have to reply. He was talking too much, justifying himself too much to let an accusation go unanswered.

"No, don't act like you don't understand me. You're lying. Making it up. You never spoke with my father's girlfriend. You don't even know anything."

"I do!" he exclaimed, "I do. She found me. She found me online, in a forum. We were discussing what it was like to grow up with parents like your father. My old man was evil. Just like yours. He used to do things to people in our small town. They vanished. No one ever found them." He chuckled now. "But I knew what happened to them. I saw where he buried them."

"You never met with my father's girlfriend," she repeated. Reverse psychology wasn't something that usually worked. The more emotionally and intellectually stable sorts saw right through it.

But now, this man yelled. "I did. I did! In fact, I recorded our meeting. Yeah, that's right. We had a call online. Over the Internet. Video. I was recording the screen." He chuckled. "Look, no, you think you're so smart, look!"

Ilse didn't want to. He was fumbling with his phone, at least this meant he was no longer playing with the knife in his pocket. He shoved it towards her, his hand shaking.

And then, she forced herself to look. An image began to move on the screen. A face she recognized.

A cold, dark sensation gripped her stomach. Icy fingers scraped down her spine.

She was now sitting, wincing at the pain in her arm. She recognized the woman.

Years and years had passed, but all of a sudden, staring at the face, she *recognized* the woman.

Her father's girlfriend. She remembered a name... Am...Amy...no... *Amelia.* A simple, plain name, to match plain face.

No makeup, like Ilse, but she wasn't pretty. A bit too large of a nose. Her jaw somewhat wobbly. But her charisma was in the eyes, and when she spoke. The video speakers were poor, but Ilse could hear the confidence.

"...my dearest's ungrateful daughter..." the voice was saying, adding a dramatic sniff. The woman shook her head, her features shifting into something of a mask. Ilse could feel her heart pound as she stared at the moving screen. More images were now flooding her mind. More horrible thoughts. She pictured that same face, smiling down concrete steps, looking over the shoulder of Ilse's father, approving of his rage.

Ilse could picture a gray scene slowly turn to color. That same woman sitting in the truck with her father, giving permission to Gerald Mueller to purchase another porcelain doll, but only in exchange for a favor.

Ilse's heart kept pounding as she watched video. The plain,

charming movements of the woman with the faint German accent. She had thin, straw-colored hair, and wore a v-neck that revealed a bit too much, including a couple of beauty marks along her cleavage. She had a simple necklace centered with a small, green stone.

"You should contact her," the woman was saying.

Ilse heard a response, this time recognizing the voice of the intruder.

"Wh—why can't I talk to you?" the voice said, a faint plea in the words. "I like you. I—I feel safe with you."

The woman on the camera leaned forward, smiling in a very motherly sort of way, and also revealing more cleavage. The juxtaposition of the image sent shivers along Ilse's arms.

"She's the one for you, my sweet," the woman in the video said. "Trust me. She'll save you. She once saved others just like you... Then again, she can be a very selfish little girl." The eyes flashed, and it almost felt as if they looked through the camera, piercing Ilse. "She can run and run in the woods. Children died because of her, you know..."

A swallowing sound. The intruder's voice. "What if... what if she doesn't want to help me?"

"Oh—sweet. Of *course* she will help you. Little Hilda wouldn't turn you down. I mean... that would make her a monster, wouldn't it?"

Ilse didn't hear a response this time, but gauging by the flow of conversation, she could picture a noncommittal nod of the head.

"Contact her tomorrow," the woman on the screen said. "And let me know how it goes. Be sure to tell her *exactly* what I told you. If she turns you down... it's as if she's killing you, isn't it?"

"Y-yes..."

"As if she's just as bad as your father." "Yes!" louder, more certain.

"Well... she has to help you. She's the only one that can save you, Kirk. We both know that, don't we?"

It was the way in which the woman spoke that most alarmed Ilse. The smooth charm, the soft, sweet delivery of dark lies that would burrow deep. Ilse didn't know how to respond. She just stared at the phone, her heart pounding horribly.

At first, she thought the video had ended. But then, she heard Kirk murmur, "So... so *how* did she kill people? She sounds awful. How can she help?"

A sigh. "She wanted to help. She was just... just too slow. So me and her father had to—"

The phone shut off.

And Ilse found her teeth pressed tightly against each other. She looked up to meet Kirk's gaze. Tears were now streaming down his face. "She... she hasn't spoken to me in a few months now," he whispered. "She told me things about you, Hilda. How much you made your daddy mad. How angry you made him. How you hurt your family by being so ungrateful... If I had..." He swallowed. "*Half* the mother you did, I would have—"

"She's not my mother," Ilse snapped, her tone frigid despite the gun. "And she's been lying to you, Kirk. Whatever she said, you can't believe."

"She told me you'd say that. And... and besides..." He sniffed. "You're the one who tried to kill me! You didn't want to help me, because you wanted me dead!"

And now, Ilse realized he was truly gone. Parroting back the lies that the woman on the phone had said.

Surprisingly, Ilse still couldn't remember the woman's last name. Only Amelia. Plain Amelia. Like porridge. Like unbuttered bread.

The woman who'd dug her hooks into Gerald Mueller. The woman who'd played puppet master for an entire family in the woods.

And now... years later, who was using another tool to torment Ilse.

She shivered, and tried slowly to push to her feet.

"Down the hall!" he snapped as she moved. "I'm warning you—don't try anything funny!"

Ilse didn't think *anything* about the situation was particularly funny. She kept her lips sealed, though, and allowed Kirk to jab the gun against her spine, pushing her forward.

She tensed, feeling the weapon against her back. She wanted to time it perfectly. To spin, snatch the weapon and disarm him. It was the only shot. She needed her gun.

But even one-armed, she wasn't sure if—

another jab. No time to hesitate—

A sudden rap of knuckles against metal.

"Doc?" a voice on the other side of the door.

Kirk froze. Ilse stiffened.

She swallowed.

"Ilse?" Tom's voice, louder now, echoing through the threshold.

Ilse winced, licking nervously at her lips.

The intruder had frozen, shifting from foot to foot. "Oh no..." he was whispering. "No, no, no..."

"Ilse, come on! I know you can hear me. Look... I—I don't have a radio. I'm not chucking pebbles at a window. But... I've got something to say! Just open up, will you?"

Ilse wanted so badly to scream. But she couldn't decide if this was the right choice. The gun was still tight in the killer's hand. He had a knife. Besides, if she didn't get the weapon first, it would put Sawyer in harm's way.

She tried to think rationally, but her mind was on fire. Desperately, she leaned back, feeling where the weapon against her spine still pressed.

"Don't you dare move," Kirk whispered in her ear. His breath smelled like cinnoman.

She felt a jolt of rage.

He'd been eating her granola.

It was *hers.* She'd made it.

He'd come into her damn home, at the behest of a wicked witch, and he'd eaten her homemade—

She spun, elbow flying. She'd gone with her bad arm, using the cast as a cudgel.

He yelled. The safety was still on with her weapon, though. She'd never seen him adjust it. Clearly, he wasn't used to handguns. Her cast slammed into the metal device. It went spinning from his grasp.

He howled like a banshee.

"Tom, intruder!" was all she managed to scream before the man tackled her from behind. She felt something sharp slashing at her throat as she hit the ground with a resounding and painful *thud.*

CHAPTER THIRTY

The gun was ten feet away, beneath the kitchen table. The knife was pressing to her throat, but she'd managed to grab the hand, gripping tight. And then, she went for a move Sawyer had taught her.

Most blades were *cutting* weapons. Slicing, gouging, stabbing. Friction was part of it. She'd seen again and again, how instructors and Sawyer had shown her to disarm a knife by *grabbing* the blade itself.

As counter intuitive as this was, if the knife wasn't given motion to slash, it wouldn't cut her.

Or so went the theory. The hours of training.

She didn't have a choice. The metal bit into her throat, so she grabbed the blade with her hand, using her broken arm to brace the wrist so he couldn't slice.

And then... With a howl.

She *twisted.*

The knife bent back in his hand. She felt the metal bite into her palm. A cut—shallow, but painful. He screamed in hear ear, and now she could hear deep *pounding* on the door. Desperate shouts from the hall.

"Doc! Ilse!" A thud against the door. Another *thud!*

Ilse struggled to keep her hold on the knife. She felt the pain in her palm intensify. Warmth trickling down her fingers now. She bucked her hips, desperately scrambling out from under the attacker's weight. But her bad hand wasn't able to maintain her grasp. He managed to pull his knife free, slicing skin.

She yelled in pain. Sawyer was screaming in the hall, his foot *thump, thump, thumping* against the metal door. But the door was designed to keep things out. She'd paid extra. The killer had bolted it.

The only way that door was opening was if someone opened it from the inside.

But candidates for this particular job were scarce. One raising his knife, threatening to plunge it into her chest.

The other with a bleeding and broken arm trying desperately to stave off the blow. She gripped his wrist, his eyes bulging beneath his silver, jutting hair. His strange, ruby tooth flashing. He tried to drive the blade down, but she held onto his wrist with all her might. Her own blood slicked his arm. Her shoulder scraped against a particularly large piece of shattered ceramics.

And then, desperate, she had a sudden idea.

She kept her grip on his wrist as he tried to drive the knife down. Then, last minute, she let go, while simultaneously jerking her head to the side.

Expecting resistance, but suddenly failing to find any, he yelped, the knife slicing down and burying into the carpet. Ilse managed to barely avoid it. With her now free hand, however, she snatched at the shard she'd felt against her shoulder.

Lifted it, sending granola chunks flying, and slahed at the killer's face.

He screamed in pain, jolting back and giving her a gap.

She surged to the side, as if going for her gun.

But the killer seemed to be expecting this. Even bleeding, screaming, he lashed out with the knife again.

But again, he missed. She wasn't going for the gun. Instead, she backed up, stumbling. The intruder, with a whole of triumph, lunged for the discarded weapon beneath the kitchen table. He snatched the gun. Raised it.

Ilse reached the door. He fumbled with it, cursing. Safety clicked.

She unbolted the door, flung it open with a shout.

The gun raised beneath the table, aiming at her. A shot. A sudden bolt of pain along her cheek, but she had dropped the moment the door open, and so he missed. The bullet sparked off the reinforced door.

She hit the ground, shouting, bleeding. Helpless.

The killer aimed at her motionless form. Even a rookie would make that shot.

He squeezed the trig—

Two loud blasts. A pause.

The killer blinked. The gun fell from his hand, striking the kitchen floor.

Sawyer stood in the doorway, his own weapon raised, breathing heavily, panic in his eyes as he stood half-crouched, as if he couldn't quite carry his full weight. He tried to take a step, but winced, grabbing at his leg. The same leg, she imagined, he'd used to batter a metal door.

He cursed, dropping suddenly, still holding his leg. "I—I think I snapped something," he murmured, his eyes fluttering.

Then, hissing through pained breaths, he stumbled towards her, reaching out, desperately scrambling for the pocket-aid pack he kept on his belt. "Hang on!" he was saying. "Shit—hang on, doc."

She shook her head numbly, sitting up, holding at her bleeding hand. "I'm fine," she murmured. "He barely scraped me."

he glanced at her hand, refusing to take her word for it. But when he saw the cut, he let out a faint shivering sigh. Still, a bandage appeared from his pocket-aid pack and he wrapped tightly around her hand.

Only then, did he glance towards the motionless form of the intruder, laying still on her kitchen floor.

"Shit," he said.

Ilse leaned back, her head pressing against the metal of the door. "I... I have a flight in three days," she muttered.

Sawyer just nodded, massaging, then wincing where his hand pressed to his knee. Like this, the two of them sat hunched in the door of her apartment. Ilse just inside, Sawyer barely in the hall, one foot across the threshold, where he kept massaging his leg. Ilse shook her head, her hair brushing against the frame.

"I... what... what did you want to say?" she said, forcing back a wince.

Sawyer glanced at her, eyes wide. He swallowed, gave a faint shake of his head, then muttered. "Later... It-it doesn't matter."

She heard the sound of shouting now from below. The buzz of the front door. Rapid footfalls. She thought she glimpsed flashing lights reflecting off the window in her small apartment.

She closed her eyes. "I... I have a flight," she murmured. "Thank you," she added.

"Now *this,*" Sawyer grunted again, still rubbing his leg. "Definitely makes us even."

She snorted, but couldn't laugh. It made her arm shake. Instead she released a faint sigh, listening to pounding footsteps, radio chatter and the flurry of first responders.

CHAPTER THIRTY ONE

Ilse was now half human and half bandage. At least, that's how she felt. She glanced down, past the bulletproof vest, staring towards her arm. It was in a much thicker cast. She wasn't sure this had been strictly necessary, but the doctor in charge had insisted, with a distrusting look in his eyes.

She'd agreed to whatever he'd said just to be given clearance to join the sting. Now, she leaned against the side of a small house in Freiburg, Germany. BKA agents crowded behind her. A young woman, an agent she'd been corresponding with before by the name of Metzger, was standing by a large, black SUV, murmuring final instructions.

Back on German soil, Ilse felt less like Hilda than she ever had before.

Except...

Except when she looked towards the small duplex at the end of the street.

He was in unit B, according to Metzger. Just waiting, watching.

She felt a flicker of unease as she stared towards the house. The windows were closed. The blinds as well. No movement. No vehicle in the drive.

She pushed from the side of the house, keeping low, approaching where Metzger continued to bark directives. "Are you sure he's in there?" she whispered as she pulled up at Metzger's elbow.

The BKA agent frowned, glancing at Ilse. "Make sure to—pardon?" She caught herself mid directive, hand lowering from her small radio. The extendable cord retracted as the shoulder mic moved back into place.

"No cars," Ilse whispered. "Are you sure he's in there? When's the last time you've had eyes on?"

Agent Metzger paused, peering over the hood of the large, black SUV, studying the small duplex. She frowned. "This morning. Five hours ago. We're good to go, Agent Beck." She paused, hesitant. "As long... as long as the information you provided—"

"It's accurate," Ilse retorted defensively. The last three days had been painful ones. Not just physically. She hadn't realized how much red tape was involved in transferring evidence from the FBI to a foreign agency. She missed the days when bureaucrats didn't control every aspect of her decision-making.

She tried not to think like this *too* often though. She didn't want to end up as jaded towards authority as Sawyer.

But still... it had taken nearly thirty hours just to see the video *herself.* The same video the intruder had shown her. Kirk Marshall, Seattle born and bred, was still something of a mystery to the FBI. They were combing through the few records they had, but were struggling to discover much about the man.

However, what she was most interested in, was the video recording of her father's girlfriend. According to the BKA, a woman was in the small duplex with Gerald Mueller.

Ilse felt certain it was the same woman from the video. The same women who had tormented her family growing up.

The video had proved particularly useful. They had, on video, from a recorded call, Amelia admitting to punishing Ilse's siblings. It wouldn't take a judge or a jury to read between the lines. She had used the phrase, "my boyfriend" which connected her to Gerald.

To Ilse, it had seemed a slamdunk. But to the BKA, it had been tentative at best.

Still, they had been desperate for new evidence to put Gerald back behind bars. While the parole board, and some of the politicians had decided it was appropriate to release the killer, the agency had different intentions for the murderer, and Ilse knew whose side she was on.

And now, after a final day of coordination before her flight, the task force was ready, the sting operation good to go.

She crouched next to her BKA liaison, eyes on the small house, the fingers on her good hand tugging uncomfortably at the bulletproof vest.

She realized this was the first time she would be involved in a case without Sawyer at her side.

She still could picture the way he had cracked two of his toes, attempting to kick down her metal door. It was the definition of stubborn. Who assaulted a metal door?

And yet she couldn't get the image out of her mind. Even after cracking his toes, he had tried to bandage her hand.

He had shot the intruder.

She shivered, remembering the way the man had attacked her in her own home.

She would move again. That much was certain.

Why not back to Germany?

There were still things for her here. She had seen the old family house, the Lakeside home, put on the market. No doubt by Gerald and his girlfriend in an attempt to fund whatever escape route they had likely planned.

She knew her father's girlfriend had spent some time in Spain. Perhaps that was where they would head eventually.

"Units ready?" said Agent Metzger at her side, using English, no doubt, for Ilse's benefit. She added something in German, which Ilse struggled to understand.

There was static on the radio, and quick responses. Ilse watched as units moved along the street, hastening forward, approaching the small duplex. Men and women with guns, wearing body armor, helmets, and even one battering ram raced behind the duplex, approaching the front door. Others, she spotted as little more than silhouettes moving through the backyard, preparing to intercept anyone that attempted to use the rear entrance.

Ilse watched, fidgeting nervously. She hadn't been cleared to participate in the breach. Because of her hand, she was required to stay back with mission command.

And yet, she felt a sudden urge to pull a Sawyer and sprint behind the breaching units.

Thankfully, she managed to keep herself in check, eyes fixed on the units. On the men and women with guns. The German agents all encroaching on the house, swarming the silent structure. Trees shifted and swayed behind the duplex. Feet thundered against concrete.

The agent at her side give a sudden barking command.

All the silence, all the faint, quiet motion suddenly erupted in sound. Men and women charged forward, yelling, shouting instructions.

Windows were smashed. A flashbang went off. Ilse watched as the metal battering ram took down the door in one shot. Two burly man stepped aside, allowing three shooters to enter behind them.

Voices called in German. They shouted, "On the floor!"

Ilse's German was rusty, but even she could pick out comments like, "Clear! Watch the side!"

For a moment, all the precision, all the planning was replaced by a sudden wild surge of motion and clatter.

Ilse watched, nibbling at her lip, and feeling even more frustrated that she couldn't join.

She shifted along the hood of the car, staring where more agents were flooding the backyard.

One thing she didn't see, however.

Her father.

Or Amelia.

No sign of an arrest. No sign of a struggle.

Which left only one option.

"Where are they?" Ilse said sharply. "I thought you said they were here this morning."

But Metzger was shaking her head, muttering quickly into the radio, issuing further instructions.

Ilse was tense. Her heart pounded. She wanted to yell. She began moving, now, indifferent to the promise she made to the German government to follow all the instructions of her supervising agent.

And to the agent's credit, she didn't stop Ilse.

More confused chatter over the radio. Police in the doorway now, shaking their heads. One of the men was still holding a handle on the metal battering ram, the back draping against the ground.

Ilse spotted figures moving along the side of the house. They were entering the second duplex door now.

Vacant, according to the BKA. No one occupied this other unit.

But now, as Ilse hastened forward and took the stairs. She peered over the shoulders of the men and women breaching the house. There was a giant hole in the wall between the two units. A hole that led from the living room of her father's place to the bedroom of the other unit.

And there, on the side of the house, she spotted disheveled earth.

Her eyes moved about this second unit. Dirt, everywhere. Buckets of dirt.

There was a shovel in one side of the room. The floor had been cut out, the concrete smashed. Then she remembered BKA's earlier reports had said her father had been watching a lot of TV. The volume loud.

But now that she thought of it, her father had never much enjoyed television.

He had been using the sounds to disguise the noises from digging.

Someone must have helped. Not just his accomplice. Someone from the outside. There was a tunnel beneath the second duplex. Now, she heard shouting. She exited the house, hastening along the side towards the backyard in the direction of the voices.

Figures were pointing.

She watched as one man in full tactical gear, irate, kicked at the ground just on the fringe of the backyard, amidst a row of trees. The forested, undeveloped lot extended further back until it met a small side street.

Now, though, the officer in the woods was pointing at the ground, his thick boot scuffing leaves. With the help of another agent, the two men lifted a camouflaged trashcan lid, covered in dust and leaves.

Ilse moved slowly, as if in a daze, and found herself peering into a dark tunnel, dirt scattered along the forest floor, pine needles and detritus scuffed where someone—or multiple someones—had clearly passed through.

She felt her stomach sink, her limp hand dangling uselessly at her side.

She should have known it was too easy. Should have known her father had something up his sleeve. When she had last visited him in prison, he had played a role. Docile, confused. But then the demon beneath had burst forth.

She should have come sooner. She had the chance nearly a week ago, but had stayed back. She could have arrived in time for the parole, maybe even swayed the board's decision. But she had tried to help Sawyer instead. Not that she regretted this decision. If not for Sawyer, she wouldn't even be alive.

But she couldn't help the slow, numb prickle of absolute fury rising from her chest. It felt as if the emotion were crawling up her throat and threatening to burst forth in a scream.

She listened, picking out phrases in German, as some of the agents began coordinating a search. APBs were called in. Other districts were notified.

But it was clear, by the frantic, desperate nature of the calls, the sheepish, disgusted way in which some of the agents stomped through the woods, kicking leaves, and studying the ground, that no one knew where her father was.

He had vanished.

She bit back another shout, and turned, fists clenched. She wasn't sure how much she would be able to do, certain that the welcome she'd been given would run dry quickly, now that the suspect who she was supposedly an expert on, had flown the coop.

The BKA agent by the SUV was waving her over, frowning, and speaking in soft tones into her shoulder mic.

Ilse brushed nervously at her hair, pushing it across her ear; she moved reluctantly back in the direction of the scowling agent.

***

Ilse sat in her borrowed vehicle, watching as the trees sped by in a blur of color.

She felt a clot in her stomach that no amount of breathing exercises seemed to release.

She had been told to return to her hotel. Seeing as she wasn't technically here with paperwork, the BKA had suggested it would save everyone a headache if she stayed where they could find her. Ilse, though, inexperienced as she was, could read between the lines. They wanted her out of their hair. They thought of her as a liability. Which, in her opinion, was hardly fair. She wasn't the one who had lost her father.

He had dug a tunnel. Under their noses, he had burrowed into his backyard.

The first spot she had told them to check was the house. Now, she imagined the place was crawling with agents. The BKA had agreed to contact her if they found anything. But nothing had yet come up.

She should have known her father wouldn't have been that predictable.

But he would need a place to lay low. Need a place to prepare for whatever the next stage of his plan was.

She drummed her fingers against the steering wheel, trying to think like her old man.

She knew she should go back to the hotel. Should let the BKA and the police handle it. Already, she had passed one roadblock.

But it didn't matter. Her mind refused to quiet. He was out there. Out there without supervision. Who knew what he was planning. Who knew what he would do next.

She shifted. Her broken wrist rested against the side of the door. Someone had reached her in her own home. Someone sent by her father's accomplice. Next, would it be Gerald himself? Would he finish what he had started all those years ago?

This thought filled her with such horror, that she couldn't help but clench her teeth.

Her eyes darted towards the green and white sign over the highway. She was supposed to take the next exit. She was supposed to head straight to the hotel.

And yet, though she couldn't quite say why she did it, she suddenly yanked the steering wheel, veering through traffic, across three lanes. Horns blared.

She spotted more than one gesture through the windshield.

But she kept her teeth set, and, watching her mirrors, turned into another offramp. She didn't know why she did it. Couldn't say besides a sudden fierce desire.

She had trusted them to keep track of her father. They were the ones who had lost him. So why on earth would she trust them again?

She picked up the pace, her frustration mounting. She needed to find where he had gone. Needed to think. She could put herself in the shoes of killers. How many murderers had she tracked? How many serial killers had she studied? So many of her victims had relied on Ilse's ability to get into the minds of their tormentors. So why couldn't she do the same with her father?

The memories were painful. But it didn't matter if she could find him. He could not be allowed to leave the country. If he disappeared, she would spend the rest of her life looking over her shoulder, wondering when there would be a gun or knife or some other weapon behind her in the dark. Wondering if she would ever be safe. Or, if her father's accomplice would hire more deranged people over the Internet to torment her, to try and kill her.

And so Ilse, feeling a rising sense of indignation, took the turn, heading back in the direction of the small town where she had grown up. The agents were at the house. Which meant her father wasn't. But where else could he be?

It wasn't like he had many friends. Wasn't like he had many options. Nor, in the many years that had passed since he been incarcerated, had he managed to find places of familiarity. Comfort, familiarity. These were the sorts of things that would appeal to a man on the run.

Not his house. That would have been too obvious.

So where?

She felt her phone vibrating. He glanced down. It was the BKA.

For a moment, she wondered if she ought to answer. But if it had been good news, they would have waited hours to tell her. It was only when they wanted something, or if they wanted her to do something, that they contacted so quickly.

Now that she had turned on the wrong ramp, she had no doubt the vehicle they had loaned her was being tracked. Likely, they wanted to know where she was going.

She ignored the phone. Sawyer really was rubbing off on her.

She kept the pace, slowing only as she reached the stop sign.

Her mind flashed back to the last time she had been in Germany. She remembered another stop sign. Remembered the small town that had slowly changed over time. A town that had been rebuilt. Many of the shops and stores and buildings looked different. But there had been one. An old building, that she still remembered.

In fact, it was one of the more clear memories she had.

As she considered it, she frowned. Where would an old killer go?

Maybe to an old store? An antique store. The same store they had often stopped at so her father could purchase his porcelain dolls. The store she had remembered sitting outside, trapped in the truck, desperate to leave.

It was the one other place she could think her father might have gone.

She lifted her phone, her fingers shaking. Perhaps she should call the BKA. Just in case.

But on the other hand, if she did, they would tell her to go back to the hotel. They would want her to hide again. Last time, she hadn't then allowed to go with them, and look what had happened.

She shook her head, tossing her phone into the back seat.

As she pulled through the stop sign, though, she let out a faint exhalations. She reached back, fishing for her phone again. She wouldn't take the call, not yet. Not unless she saw something. But she could at least keep the phone on her. It wasn't like she even knew if her hunch would yield any fruit.

She simply couldn't shake the image in her mind of the truck, her father, and Amelia sitting in the passenger seat, egging Gerald on.

Ilse grit her teeth, and hastened through the small town. Trees and greenery sheltered most the houses, and even the shops. It was as if someone had plucked a small section of civilization from the map and placed it smack dab in a forest.

There had been a time, when Ilse might have thought a place like this was charming. But those thoughts rarely lasted. She had too many memories amidst the trees. To much baggage.

And then, ahead, she spotted the familiar antique store. There were no cars in the parking lot. Was the store closed? It was still only afternoon.

Slowly, she rolled into the parking lot, glancing towards the other shops framing the antique store.

A couple of people were sipping coffee in a café. One man was sorting through laundry, talking to someone out of sight that she couldn't see through the window.

Her eyes moved back to the antique store. A small sign in the window read, *closed.*

But then, her eyes moved to the posted hours in small, peeling white letters on the glass.

It wasn't supposed to close until evening.

She approached the door, her reflection cast by the glass. Within, she spotted some old furniture, a small cupboard and a marble counter curved in an L-shape. Beyond, further back in the dark, dingy space, she noted a large cabinet filled with small tchotchkes. She'd been through before, and at the time, an older gentleman had chased her from his place.

Locals still remembered the Mueller house, and the horrors within.

She pressed her face against the glass, her breath fogging the surface. She frowned, peering into the dark.

No movement. No visible disturbance. Everything neat, in order, perfectly arranged.

What if she was wrong? What if her father *hadn't* come here?

She felt a strange chill down her arms to the tips of her fingers. She winced, adjusting her damaged arm in its cast and using this to knock against the door.

"Hello!" she called, her voice sound small even to her own ears. "Hello? Can anyone hear me?"

She couldn't remember the name of the store owner. Couldn't remember much of anything save the brief glimpses of memory flashing through her mind's eye.

But again, no response.

She felt a flicker of frustration, and knocked against the glass, louder this time.

But it was like screaming at a tomb.

No motion. No response.

Only dead silence.

Hesitantly, she pushed her hand against the door.

Locked.

That, of course, would have been too easy. And when had her life ever been easy?

She began to move around the side of the antique store, stepping down the small wooden steps and moving between the alley formed by the bakery she'd spotted earlier and strange, old shop her father had once loved so dearly.

As she moved, her brow furrowed.

The side door was shut as well. But there, in the middle of the wall, above a garbage can, she spotted an open window.

Her mind darted back to the garbage lid used to disguise the tunnel exit.

Of course, *this* particular bin still had its lid. Slowly, tentatively, she clambered on top. "Hello?" she called into the dark space. No response. The window remained open, gaping at her, almost like a half-shuttered eye mid-wink.

But what coy secrets lingered on the other side of the glass?

Her reflection frowned. She tried the door handle to the side entrance, leaning across the garbage can... Also locked.

She shot a look over her shoulder, peering down the alley.

No witnesses. No cars in the parking lot. Faintly, she thought she heard voices from the direction of the bakery. Cheerful prattle.

No one was watching her, though.

Did she really think her father had come to hide in an antique store? What would have been the point?

Familiarity. Comfort.

She knew the answer well enough. A place to regroup. A place to lay low that had minimal foot traffic. Even the sign out front was peeling, suggesting that attracting new customers wasn't the aim of the small shop.

Now, lingering on the bin, she wrinkled her nose, waving a hand against the odor of refuse rising. She let out a faint sigh of frustration, realizing she'd already made her decision.

Nothing for it...

She slipped through the gap in the window, wiggling her shoulders to lift the frame a bit further. Faint trails of dust dislodged trickling along her neck, down her shirt collar. She resisted the urge to sneeze as she pulled herself through, and—blinking in a dark, small storage space—she landed on the ground with quiet movements.

As she adjusted, blinking, trying to see clearly in the poorly illuminated space, she went suddenly still.

A man was lying on the ground, a gag around his lips. His hands bound behind his back. An old man, with wispy hair. A brown newsboy cap angled off to the side against his cheek, where it looked to have fallen from his head.

He was mumbling through his gag, kicking and shifting, and attempting—desperately--to gain her attention.

Ilse crawled forward, her pulse quickening, small pinpricks prickling across her arms.

"Quiet," she whispered in German. She wasn't sure if she'd used the right word, but the man seemed to get the gist. He went still.

She felt certain now she recognized him as the shop owner. With shaking fingers on her single good hand, she began to tug and pull at the ropes binding the older gentleman's wrists.

And then, through a small door behind the old man, she heard voices.

She tensed. The man on the ground began wriggling furiously.

Ilse stared, eyes the size of saucers, as a shadow moved beneath the door, shifting across the gap of light.

"I heard something," a voice said in German.

A familiar, gregarious voice. The voice of someone practiced in charm, in placation. But a voice Ilse knew not to trust.

The voice of Amelia, who's last name she still didn't know—the woman who'd convinced Kirk to attack her.

Ilse felt her stomach fall to her toes as she shuffled back, moving towards the open window. On either side of her, she spotted metal shelves stacked with small, dusty items. Likely some of the more expensive wares of the small antique shop, kept behind lock and key.

Now, however, serving as the prison for their proprietor.

The shadows continued to shift under the door, and Ilse slowly moved around the back of the metal shelves. She kept a finger to her lips, her eyes wide where she met the gaze of the bound store owner. He kept emitting muffled sounds through his gag, shaking his head, his eyes ringed with red.

A sudden *click.* The door slowly opened.

Ilse's heart lodged in her throat. She shifted into the shadows behind the shelf, using a small, porcelain jar as her primary form of camouflage. And then, the door to the supply close was opened.

Ilse stared a the face of the woman...

Older than the recording on the video. More lines, less fat. She'd lost weight, but this had caused her skin to sag. Now, cruel eyes surveyed the small space. They landed on the store owner, blinked owlishly, then moved on as if he were nothing more than a spare carpet.

Ilse tried to crouch lower as the woman's gaze swept towards her.

And then, a second silhouette appeared in the door. Ilse stared, bug-eyed, as her father appeared. Gerald Mueller's graying hair crowned features that were just shy of handsome. He had sharp cheekbones and a rounded chin that made him look almost feminine in certain light. But the man she remembered was far *larger,* far *stronger.* This man...

This strange specimen standing in the door, behind his female accomplice, as if he were frightened of the bound victim, didn't have the same effect.

Ilse watched them both, her eyes peering through shadow, fixated on the figures. She felt a slow chill along her spine... but also, she realized, she'd forgotten to breath. The dust from the old items lingered in the air, threatening to irritate her airways. She closed her eyes, briefly, blinking aside a faint stinging sensation.

All the while, her mind whispered things...

Memories accompanied accusations.

She cowered in a dark corner, hiding in shadow as the two tormentors from her childhood stood over a helpless man.

She thought of her siblings. Thought of how much she'd ignored, avoided. How often she pretended she couldn't hear the pain... Didn't see the abuse. She remembered stumbling through the woods. Remembered returning to her family *late.* Very late.

And now, Ilse's stomach twisted. It was happening again.

Her crouched, small... hidden. Scared.

And those two standing over a victim, as if they had all the time in the world, as if nothing they'd done even bothered them. Ilse felt a flicker of rage.

She wondered if this was how Sawyer had felt when marching into that prison.

She realized something else now... she'd been operating on pure instinct, crouching in a hiding spot. But now...

Now as she stared at the figures in the door, her good hand moved to her holster. Her right hand was still in a cast, which meant her left now touched against her weapon on her off-hip. She was *not* a shooter. Certainly not with her left hand.

But why was she hiding in the dark?

Why cower? *She* had the gun. She was the one who'd come hunting *them.* Gone was little Hilda Mueller.

Ilse Beck had now taken her place.

She wasn't even listening to the two of them, now. Rather, like a wraith in a graveyard, she slowly emerged from behind the shelf, straightening. Her eyes never left her father. She stared at those familiar features, remembering how often she'd only felt terror. Remembering how often she'd gone to bed shaking, waking up to worse nightmare sunder the sun than those experienced under her covers.

She pulled her weapon from her hip, emerging behind the shelf, aiming over the bound store owner.

Except as she stepped forward, it wasn't a strange, older man she saw laying prone on the cold floor. She pictured her siblings... her mind darted to little Kat. To Heidi... She thought of how many members of her family had ended up...

Brothers dead. One scared of his own shadow. Their youngest sister in an insane asylum. Another sister had tried to kill Ilse. Also now dead.

And amidst it all, there was Hilda Mueller.

"Put your hands where I can see them," Ilse said slowly, her voice shaking.

She emerged fully from behind the metal shelves, gun pointed towards her father's face, darting towards his girlfriend's form. "Don't move a muscle."

They both went very still, staring at here, eyes wide. She let out a shaking little breath. Somehow... this didn't feel like she'd imagined it would. No sense of satisfaction. No sense of justice.

Just fear... and deep, deep sadness.

How many women longed to point weapons at their only surviving parent? This wasn't a reunion... it was a tragedy.

And there was absolutely nothing she could do to rewrite a history her father had penned in blood.

"Who—what—" Amelia stammered, but then her eyes suddenly widened in recognition.

Gerald Mueller just looked confused, blinking in the dark and glancing at the gun in her hand as if unsure what it was.

CHAPTER THIRTY TWO

Ilse then spoke, in a slow, cold tone. "Hands up, both of you. Don't even flinch."

She emerged fully from behind the stock shelves, stepping in front of the window she'd entered through. Her eyes flicked from her father's accomplice to the man himself, her heart pounding. Small bursts of sheer hatred sparked through her. She stared at Gerald Mueller—the old version of her childhood tormentor.

Not everyone is given the chance to face their bogeyman, the monster in their closet.

And now, up close, it wasn't as imppressive as she remembered.

He was smaller than she recalled. Awkward. He fidgeted where he stood. Every so often, Gerald glanced at Amelia, muttering beneath his breath.

"He's not well," Amelia snapped. "Have a heart.

Her tone was wheedling, but severe. The plain-faced woman stared at Ilse over the barrel of the gun as if the weapon wasn't even there. As if all that stood between the two of them were the words yet spoken.

Ilse had no interest in a conversation, though.

"Untie him!" she snapped. "Do it!"

Her father was still staring blankly. Again, most likely playing a role. *He's not well...* What did Amelia mean? Not that Ilse cared one way or another. The woman's attempt to wheedle sympathy was somewhat laughable given the man they'd tied up and left on the floor.

"Come on!" Ilse snapped, wishing her left hand hadn't been trembling so badly. "Hurry up!" She waved her weapon towards the store owner once more.

Slowly, her father's companion lowered to a knee, though her eyes never left Ilse. Then, in a quick motion, a knife suddenly appeared in Amelia's hand.

"Hey!" Ilse yelled.

"For the ropes! Just the ropes!" said the woman quickly, her eyes widening. "Don't... just, calm down, Hilda..."

It was the name that did it.

That woman, using Ilse's childhood name... She felt a sudden surge of unrelenting fury. She yelled, her voice carrying. "Do *not* call me that!"

Amelia shook her head, slowly cutting at the ropes binding the old man. Ilse's eyes fixed on the blade. She'd decided if it moved within a foot of anything vital, she would open fire. She didn't think she was thinking particularly rationally, but at the same time, Ilse wanted to control the situation. She also wanted to make a call.

But it was difficult to keep a gun raised *and* reach for a phone while one-handed. She felt a flash of frustration as she shifted, feeling the weight of the phone in her pocket, watching small strands of rope fiber tumble to the floor and gather in a small clump. And then, the mans' wrists were cut free.

He scrambled to his feet, quick at first, but then slower as age had its say.

Gerald Mueller continued to watch in the back, still looking shellshocked.

"What's wrong with him?" Ilse said at last, pointing the gun towards her father. "Why isn't he talking?"

Amelia's eyes narrowed, flashing with something bordering contempt. "He has alzheimer's. Not that you'd care."

"No. You're right. I don't."

"You never cared much for anyone but yourself, Hilda." Amelia slowly pushed a hand against her knee, preparing to prop herself up.

"Did I say you could rise?" Ilse snapped.

Her father's friend froze, swallowing and staring. "Are you going to shoot me?"

Ilse glanced to the window, but then back into the room. She felt deeply unsatisfied. Why wasn't her father speaking? This wasn't how it was meant to go...

"I should," she said, biting her lip. "After everything you've done."

"What we've done?" Amelia said, stunned. "How—how *dare* you!"

Ilse blinked at the fury in the words.

"After everything you've put poor Gerald through? He's now gone and lost his mind!"

She scoffed. "That I put him through? He did this to himself."

"You ungrateful little girl!" the woman exclaimed, her voice rising an octave. "You're not well, Hilda. You cost your father twenty years—for what? Lies? Lies you made up! You always were a liar, telling the neighbor children such awful stories. But your father—such a good man—he loved you so much. He wanted to take care of you. I told him to put you in an instutition. I admit I did. I wasn't as strong as your father. But he insisted on keeping you safe. Keeping you away from others—especially after you nearly drowned that little boy."

Ilse just stared at Amelia. "Do you honestly think you're going to gaslight me?" she said.

"Gaslight? It's true, dear. We only wanted what was best for you. The most expensive doctors and pscyhologists. They alll came to speak with you. None of them saw hope. And then one day, you made up such a *giant* lie that the police came and took my Gerald away. Because of your lies, you cost me years with my love. I hope you understand, Hilda," Amelia said in a long-suffering, gently scolding sort of tone. "That words have power. And yours hurt the people who loved you most."

"That's love, is it? Torturing children in a basement?"

"Children?" She shook her head, wrinkling her nose in confusion. "There were no children. Only *you.*"

"What do you think you're playing at?" Ilse said. "I know what happened. I remember everything. Even your name, Amelia."

The woman didn't flinch. She just gave a small, sad sigh. "You're suffering an episode, dear. You're not well. Have you been taking your medicine?"

"Shut up. I mean it."

"You would pretend to have friends in that basement. Pretend to have brothers and sisters. But it was all make-believe. You know that, don't you? You *must* know that."

"I said *shut up.*"

"And there we were, listening to long nights of your screaming, your crying. Listening as you wailed. We tried to let you live in the room upstairs, but you scratched and kicked until your fingers and toes were bloody until we let you back into the basement. It was the only way we knew how to calm you, dear. My lovely, little *Hilda.*"

"Get on the ground! Do it now."

Amelia did not comply. She shook her head, and in fact started rising slowly, a soft, pitying look in her eyes. "Hilda... please... You know me. Remember how I would tuck you in at night? Singing your favorite song? Remember when I would bring you ice cream during thunderstorms and we would snuggle together, listening to the rain? This isn't like you, Hilda... Put the weapon down. You're going to hurt someone and do something you deeply regret.

Ilse was beginning to lose her patience.

None of the comments were landing, or leaving their mark. If anything, the sheer brazenness of the baldfaced lies only angered her further. She was sick of these people—of how they thought they could get away with murder. She was no longer a child.

Now she came to this conversation as someone trained in the very field Amelia was leveraging. It was a pathetic, weak attempt to gain some sort of pyschological control. But Ilse wasn't going to bite. She said, slower, her voice firm, "Stop moving, and sit down. *Now!*"

Her hand was no longer trembling, her finger taught on the trigger.

And suddenly, two things happened.

First, Amelia began to speak again. The same, simpering, condescending tone she'd been using up to this point. But before she could form her thought, her boyfriend reacted.

"Ah shit," he said. "Sorry, Am—"

And then he shoved Amelia from behind, sending her stumbling towards Ilse. He subsequently slammed the door, and Ilse heard the sound of thumping footsteps as he made good his getaway.

Amelia scrambled for the weapon as she regained her balance. But what the woman thought she posessed in words, she certainly lacked in physique. Ilse dropped her gun, letting it fall, then grabbed the woman's arm, twisted. The knife fell along with the gun, clattering.

The shopkeeper yelled. Ilse turned her father's girlfriend in one motion, shoving her against the shelves. She put her knee in the woman's back, holding her in place. "Don't move a muscle!" Ilse snapped. And then she pulled the cuffs from her belt, quickly—or as quickly as possible given her use of one arm—cuffed the woman, looping the chain through the metal shelf.

"Don't—what do you think, you're doing. Hilda, Hilda it's me—oomph."

Ilse shoved the woman out of the way, already moving in pursuit of her father. She stopped long enough to secure her firem. She pointed a finger at the shopkeeper. "Call the police! Now! Don't let her free-whatever you do. Keep her here until they come!"

The man nodded fiercely, his eyes wide in panic.

And then Ilse raced past him, her footsteps like a rainstorm against the floor. She flung open the storage closet's door, and raced into the dusty shop. Her father had already reached the front door, his fingers scrambling with the locks. He shot panicked looks over his shoulder in her direction.

Gone was the look of confusion. Gone was his air of mental fog.

Now, alert, frightened, he flung himself through the door, and swung it shut behind him.

Ilse gave chase. She vaulted a slick counter, landed on the other side, nearly toppling a rack of postcards. She hurtled another display case full of small, ceramic cats, and then hotfooted out of the front door in hot pursuit.

She spotted her father, racing between the buildings, doubling back and using the same alley she had, as if they shared the same instincts. The thought that she shared anything with that hated man made her skin crawl.

Forced to holster her weapon now, she wished she'd been given a radio—something to rapidly communicate. But BKA hadn't expected her to need one, and she didn't have the time to stop and make a phone call.

With a desperate shout, she rushed down the side alley, following in her father's footsteps.

He had reached the back of the commercial buildings now, the dumpsters in his wake. One toppled box—as if it had once belonged to a large wardrobe—was now shoved on its side. Thin, wooden and cardboard support was being used to help Gerald Mueller over the chainlink fence set against the forest.

Long branches reached down as if attempting to keep the man at bay. But determinedly, with a survival instincts born of desperation, he clambered over the metal fence. The rattling of the fence sounded like wind chimes as he gave a loud grunt and hit the forest floor.

He took a moment to look back, eyes full of panic.

He stared through the gaps in the fence, his gaze meeting hers. Ilse's hand darted to her weapon as she rushed towards the toppled wardrobe box.

Her father swallowed, giving a faint shake of his head. He opened his mouth as if to say something. For a brief second, Ilse wondered if he might grovel. Might apologize, even. She wasn't sure what to expect.

But then his lips curled into a sneer—a very familiar expression. And he turned, racing into the woods, scattering detritus. One-armed, it took some effort to navigate the wardrobe box. She finally reached the top, slipped over the metal bar, and, with a wince, dropped to the other side.

Her feet hit the forest floor, but buckled. She sprawled across the ground, but mercifully managed to keep hold of her weapon.

Leaves fluttered as she pushed roughly back to her feet. Her heart pounded as she shoved between the trees and moved in the direction she'd seen her father flee. The sounds of the forest seemed duller, muted somehow.

Her injured arm struck a low-hanging branch, and she hissed, stumbling to the side as small boughs tugged at her. Her body armor shifted uncomfortably, feeling more like an obstacle. She resisted the urge to remove it, however.

Was her father armed?

Had he managed to grab something to defend himself in his escape?

She pressed her teeth tightly together, hastening forward with each stumbling step. Leaves scattered. The floor cushioned the sound of her movements, but emitted faint *crunching* noises.

Ahead, she heard similar sounds. Glimpsed her father's figure moving hastily away. She also detected the faint sounds of him gasping, desperate, drawing air with reluctant lungs.

She couldn't imagine he'd spent very *much* time exercising in prison.

She gained on him, rushing through the trees, eyes fixated on him.

She remembered another time, as a child, desperate, fleeing this very man's home and hastening into the woods. She remembered bare feet, painful steps. The sheer cold and hunger and thirst threatening to consume her.

She remembered getting lost. Remembered struggling to find her way back...

She remembered the terror of the forest.

But now, *she* was the terror in the forest.

Her father tripped, hitting the ground. He cursed and rose again in a shower of leaves. Still, she kept coming. Closing the distance. Fifty feet. Thirty.

He shot furious looks over his shoulder, his gaze burning, but also tinged with terror.

She was smaller than him. Thin. She wasn't someone who prided herself on an impressive physique.

The small, thin woman was running down the big bad wolf.

And then she was on him. He snarled as she drew within striking distance, flinging a hand back. It carried a sharp stone he'd picked up from the ground. She avoided this, though. He stumbled, grabbed a branch and tried to brandish it. The thing still had small branches and many leaves. He tried to crack this in half to give himself something of a spear.

But she barreled into him and sent him to the ground. The makeshift stick went flying. He struggled, scrambling back, but she was already on her feet. He swiped at her again, but missed.

He was yelling now. Another flail...

Another miss...

She wasn't even moving that much. He was just so slow, so weak. So old.

His fingers grazed her cheek as he tried to grab at her face. The sensation of his skin against hers sent shivers down her spine. She yelled in revulsion, avoiding him by stepping back.

Gun now in her hand.

She pointed the weapon at her childhood tormentor. At the boogeyman who haunted her dreams.

She felt her chest rising and falling. Felt a surge of rage well up within her.

This, she knew, was how Sawyer must have felt when walking into that prison.

They were in the woods. Alone... Nothing to watch them except for the trees.

Her father had collapsed against a tree, sliding down. His own efforts to attack her had taxed his energy. Now, he was in misery. He let out a huffing breath, a flickering sigh. Gerald Mueller was gasping, crawling back, emitting a rustling sound with each panicked motion. "No, no, Heidi," he whispered, shaking his head. "Please... please, have mercy!"

He hadn't even called her by her name.

"Heidi is dead," Ilse said simply, her tone flat. Her emotions were fading. How often had she lived by putting herself in others' shoes? Trying to find the right thing to do... To find compassion for even the most damaged sorts.

Now, though, this part of her was temporarily on reprieve.

All she felt was rage.

A pure, unadulterated rage. A rage she felt *entitled* to.

And there he was, pathetic, mumbling. He didn't even recognize his own daughter. He'd been just as bad when she'd visited him in prison.

But now, staring at him, she wondered in those vacant, pleading eyes, if she glimpsed a spark of *truth* to what Amelia had said.

Her father's health was declining...

If she put two bullets in his skull, this would certainly be the case.

Her hand continued shaking, her body poised, tense, her teeth pressed together.

He was mewling like some abandoned creature. His eyes burdened with tears. He sobbed, shaking his head. She wondered when someone crossed a line... when they went from salvagable to *too-far-gone.* She knew it wasn't her choice to make, though.

She bit her lip.

And yet...

Her finger was the only steady part of her hand. The wrist was shaking... but the finger on the trigger was resolute.

Such a simple squeeze.

A quarter inch of movement and it would solve so many problems for everyone...

It would put an end to the torment she endured at night.

Just a small motion.

"P-Please, Heidi," he whispered, shaking his head. His eyes were once again darting side to side, as if he were confused. As if he didn't know where he was.

But was he faking.

Ilse swallowed. If she shot him, she would be the one behind German bars.

But she didn't care in that moment. If she shot him, she'd also be the one who put an end to this horror. The woman who killed the monster.

"P-please..." he whispered.

She thought of her words to Sawyer, back outside the prison. But her placations seemed small, hollow things now. She didn't know if she even believed in what she'd done...

Perhaps she should have let Tom kill that man in prison. Given him the vengeance he'd so desperately desired.

The same vengeance that she now had served on a plate.

She barely recognized this old, decrepit version of her father, though. Now... she watched as he turned, trying to crawl, belly in the leaves, face down. He made it as far as a root.

"Don't," she said simply.

He went as still as ice, breathing in shallow puffs.

Then he didn't move at all, only faintly trembling whenever he heard a sound in the woods.

And then came the *click.*

He tensed.

But she'd only adjusted her grip on the weapon.

She breathed heavily, staring at where her father lay motionless on the floor, as if dead. Playing possum...

That's what he'd once called it.

Though when he'd said it, his voice had carried all colors of contempt. He'd stared at the children, pretending to be asleep beneath their sleeping bags. His voice had bristled as he'd shouted to rouse them, accusing them of thinking he was stupid. His temper had led to more than one beating that day.

Ilse stared at the man who'd injured her ear with scissors. Who'd killed her siblings. Who'd attacked, abused, belittled, broken her family.

Stared at the man who now lay facefirst in the leaves, lips pressed to the ground.

She felt no sense of satisfaction.

Not even a sense of justice.

Her weapon trembled in her hand, but she lowered it slowly, with a fluttering sigh and a shake of her head. With the new evidence from the recorded phone call the postcard-sender had provided, plus the kidnapping of the antique store owner, her father would head back to prison.

And even this gave her no satisfaction.

She was a therapist. She'd been trained to *fix* broken things. What sort of satisfaction could possibly be found when staring at the most broken of any she'd encountered.

A figure who'd spread that brokenness to others.

He'd never sought help. Never asked. He'd enjoyed his little kingdom of torment in the basement of that small home.

And now... he was going back to prison. Two of his sons dead. A daughter dead. Others that daughter had killed dead. Mountains of trauma and pain and lost potential in the rest of his surviving relatives. A veneer of fear and distrust over a once-idyllic town.

This was his legacy.

The greatest punishment for a man like this, Ilse pondered, was his sheer existence.

On the other hand... she wasn't proud to think it... but she hoped this time they locked him up and threw away the key.

In the distance, she heard the whir of sirens. Her father didn't react, didn't move. She leaned back, shoulders against a tree trunk, feeling the rough wood at her spine. She let out a faint sigh. And suddenly, her phone buzzed.

Slowly, with the fingers from her broken wrist—so she could keep her gun at the ready—she withdrew her phone. A difficult task, but once done, she glanced down. Not the BKA.

Sawyer.

She hesitated, staring at the small speech bubble. Clicked it.

Hey doc, the text read. *Miss me yet? I had a locksmith come by. They reinforced your door. Installed a doorcam and a monitor in your house as well, but it's tied to your phone, so only you have access. Will have to wait until you're here to activate it...*

She blinked in surprise as she read this. She hadn't been expecting Sawyer to do any of that. Looking out for her, like always. Another thing she also realized... The idea of anyone, especially a man, tampering with her locks, with her door while she was gone would have severely bothered her...

Anyone except Tom. He felt... safe.

Like family?

No... no, far, far better than *her* family. She scowled at the man in the leaves. She didn't think twice about having Sawyer install a security system. If anything, she trusted his experience in that area more than hers.

Then again... she was going to move. She couldn't imagine staying in that place. Maybe back to her lakeside home?

She noticed another notification on her phone.

As if sensing her mood, as only phones and their corporate advertisers seemed to manage, there was an ad open.

An advertisement for another lakeside home. One she'd been looking at earlier.

The small, cramped, abandoned house only a fifteen minute drive from where she currently stood.

The lakeside, family home.

A place once filled with nightmares... But now... She wondered if perhaps this was a sign. Maybe staying in Germany was the path forward. She might be able to reconnect with some of her surviving family. Though they'd made it clear they wanted nothing to do with her.

At the very least, she could rebuild that old home. With Gerald or Amelia or one of their lackeys at large, perhaps things could be redeemed, restored, healed... Or perhaps just burned to the ground... The earth salted.

But this had always been the most difficult part. Grieving pain meant admitting it couldn't be restored. She couldn't *get* those years back... But what if... what if she turned the home into something useful? A place for the hurting, the broken... maybe a counselor's office?

She frowned, considering this.

And only then did she realize... for at least a full minute...

Not a single thought had gone in the direction of her father where he grovelled in the leaves. Not a single moment was spared for the man who haunted her dreams.

She smiled at this, lowering her phone, listening as the sirens wailed, and waiting for backup to arrive.

CHAPTER THIRTY THREE

Ilse listened, doing her best to pick up the words in German lobbed back and forth across the hood of the vehicle. The windows were tinted. Her father and his accomplice sitting in the back of the car. Both of them cuffed, the doors sealed.

Ilse didn't want to stand this close to a car with her father in it, but she also knew if she strayed too far, there was a chance Agent Metzger, who was embroiled in a debate with her superior, would send someone to cuff and drag her back.

So Ilse simply waited, twisting nervously, her back to the vehicle.

Occasionally, she was able to pick out phrases.

"...Why wasn't anyone accomponying her?" This came from the tall, pale-haired woman with a pinched face and severe expression.

Metzger replied, "She went on her own."

"That doesn't answer my question."

"We have him, don't we?"

"Have him on what?"

The convesation continued in more muted tones as the two figures moved around the front of the vehicle, fingers waving, voices rising then falling. Every so often one of the BKA agents would glance in Ilse's direction, and she tried to force a sufficiently chagrined expression.

Difficult, this.

She would have done it all the same again.

And now, with her father in cuffs inside the SUV, she wanted to leave the scene behind, to simply march away and never look back.

At last, though, as Ilse began edging away, Metzger called out. "Beck! One moment..." The agent moved towards Ilse, frowning as she came, clearly feeling the sting of her supervisor's gaze burning between her shoulders.

Ilse felt numb as the woman approached. Exhausted, even, wanting nothing more than to curl up in a bed with a nice book and allow the weight of the world to finally melt from her shoulders.

Now, though, as Metzger approached, the woman was frowning, her dark features creased in shadow as her perfectly manicured brow twitched between flavors of disapproving and downright angry.

"You did not return to the hotel," said Metzger as she came to a stop in front of Ilse. The woman brushed her hair behind an ear, standing with one foot angled off.

"I had a lead, so I took it," Ilse said. "Like I told you; I didn't know he'd be there."

"How come you didn't call? Didn't notify *anyone?"* Metzger didn't glance back towards the tall, pale-haired woman by the car, but she didn't need to for Ilse to guess these questions and their tenor were partially meant for the spectator.

"I can't say," Ilse murmured. She shrugged. "I didn't know where he was. I thought I had a chance... I..." She wasn't being coherent. And she knew that. She stared determinedly at Metzger refusing to glance in the direction of the parked SUV.

"They're in custody, aren't they?" Ilse said at last with a very Sawyer-esque shrug. "The man they'd bound is safe. I believe you owe me a thank you. Not a lecture."

She also spoke loud enough for the silver-haired supervisor to overhear. Her words only received a deeper frown, but then a long sigh. The supervisor shook her head, shifting and lifting her phone.

Metzger glanced back at her boss, then returned her look to Ilse. Her features softened a bit now that they weren't being watched.

"Well done," Metzger said simply. "Perhaps not by the book... but..." she shrugged, then shook her head, running a hand through her hair. "Thank you," she said simply, her voice dropping to nearly a whisper. She shot a look over her shoulder towards where her supervisor was waiting, a phone to her cheek, but the glare having returned.

"I... thank you," Ilse said simply, giving a quick nod.

"You, of course, are welcome to help in the interrogations," said Metzger. "We won't start until tomorrow, though. They've lawyered up, and there's a bit of a hassle since we're arresting a man recently released on parole. But... if you can stay another few days..."

She trailed off, allowing Ilse to fill in the blanks.

Which Ilse did, considering this.

A few more days...

Maybe even longer?

But what was there for her, here...

Did she really want to interrogate the man? Sit across from him in a cold, dingy room, asking him questions he would only lie to?

If there was nothing to stay for, though... What was there to return for?

She smiled towards Metzger... It wasn't a humorous look, nor a friendly smile. More like a smile of resignation. An acknowledgment that she had nothing left in the tank.

"I'll... I'll think about it. My flight is supposed to leave tomorrow evening."

Metzger nodded. "We could use your help. By the book this time," she added, more firmly.

And then she turned on her heel, moving hastily back towards her waiting supervisor.

Ilse watched her leave, then, limbs heavy, turned towards the street and a waiting vehicle.

CHAPTER THIRTY FOUR

It had been a difficult, painful decision to leave it all behind. She stood outside the restaurant, shifting uncomfortably in the floral dress she'd purchased. It hung to her ankles, and had sleeves. Even the neck was cut high. She wasn't sure if she'd ever seen so much fabric on a dress.

This, though, was what had attracted her to the thing. She paused to glance at her reflection in the glass, frowning. She looked like a clown. Too much damn makeup...

Lipstick too. Gah.

She resisted the urge to spin on her heel and march back towards the taxi that had brought her. She'd drawn the line at piercing her ears.

Not that he'd asked for any of it. She just...

In a way had wanted to make a new impression. A fresh start.

Germany... Germany was old news. Her childhood was gone. There was no rebuilding it. But the scattered ashes of the immolated years were now the solid foundation upon which she was determined to build.

And she *had* been building.

This was the part that struck her.

As much as she didn't want to admit it, she'd been living in the past. Sometimes, there was no other way to live. But other times, it made things... opaque. Bleary. A befogging, obfuscating approach to the future.

With her father and his accomplice both in BKA custody, both facing charges not only for kidnapping the antique store's owner, but also threatening his life, Ilse felt as if she could see things more clearly.

The idea of purchasing her childhood home was a fanciful one.

And now...

Now she pushed through the glass door, stepping into the restaurant. Soft music met her ears, and a warm breeze swirled out to meet the night.

She glanced around the small space, eyes darting from one table to the next. She shifted uncomfortably, wondering if her lipstick was too dark. If her eyes were too laden in mascara. Shit... She'd watched like six videos online to try and get the application perfectly.

Maybe he wouldn't like this anyway. Maybe he was going to think she was trying too hard...

She sighed, letting out a faint huff, summoning almost as much courage as had been required to slip through that window in the back of the store.

And then, biting her lip, she marched forward.

Agent Tom Sawyer sat in the back of the restaurant. A small paper napkin had been torn to shreds and now encircled his empty plate. The ice water jug, with lemon wedges, was nearly empty. And Sawyer's glass had already been used.

She fidgeted as she slipped behind a wooden chair. "Sorry," she murmured sheepishly.

And then she reached Sawyer, pausing behind the chair. He looked up at her. His hair was combed, now. And his baseball cap was nowhere to be seen. In fact, he was wearing a black tuxedo. She glanced around the restaurant. He'd said, when she'd agreed to his offer, that it was a high end place.

Now that she looked, though, most people were dressed cocktail casual. Whatever that meant.

Sawyer was clearly out of his element, and she wondered how long it had been since the last time he'd dressed up for a date... But there was something almost comforting about the strange wardrobe choice. She was similarly out of her depth. But when his eyes landed on Ilse, he suddenly brightened. He looked away from the torn pieces of napkin, grinning up at her. Just as quickly, though, he hid his grin as if worried this might offend.

He watched her, then cleared his throat. "Holy shit," he said.

A woman sitting with a child two tables away shot him a frown.

He winced. "Sorry," he muttered, glancing at his plate. He cleared his throat. "Umm... Wow. You look..."

"Too much," Ilse said. She winced. "I—I just... I was trying something new. And... you know what, I can go wash off—"

"—Amazing—"

"—in the bathroom, wait, what?"

"—No, don't go wash—"

"You think I look amazi—"

"Wait, sorry. No, you go first."

Ilse and Sawyer both stopped, drawing quick breaths. Things had been so comfortable between them. So easy. Now, though, Ilse felt as if something had changed.

This wasn't the easy-going banter in the field. Wasn't Sawyer's usual deadpan, single-syllable words accompanied by her patient clarifications.

She thought as she stood awkwardly, that she detected an unfamiliar aftershave. Not his usual sandalwood shampoo. She shook her head, trying not to think about *smelling* the man. Dear God. What if he could read her thoughts?

Why did people do this for fun? Public embarrassment. That was what she'd signed up fo—

Sawyer was on his feet, moving quickly around the table and pulling out her chair. At least it didn't scrape *too* loudly against the ground. But as he did it, he smiled, flashing her a quick wink. At the familiar gesture, she found she could breath a bit easier. Slowly, she lowered into the offered seat.

"Thank you," she murmured.

"You look great. Like really. I mean, you always do, but... yeah. Great."

Ilse hid a smile, nodding as he circled back to sit across from her. She noticed he'd eaten the breadsticks as well.

"How long have you been waiting?" she asked, glancing up.

"Oh," he said uncomfortably. "Umm..."

"Was I late?"

"No, no. You're on time. I just... got here early is all. It's been a while, you know. I haven't done something like this in... ten years? Eight? I don't remember."

She nodded, watching him. Behind, she spotted images playing on a television screen along the bar. A news feed. She frowned, watching as a television presenter began flashing images across the screen. The small, white scroll at the bottom read, *stunning escape of German convict leads to new secrets from decades-old case.*

She wrinkled her nose. Flanking this television was another one showing a golf game and another displaying some cooking show. It all seemed so pedestrian when displayed so closely together.

She didn't like how it looked. For a moment, she considered going over and asking them to turn of the televisions.

But then, Sawyer glanced at his menu and muttered. "No burgers."

"Sorry, what?"

He winced, shaking his head. "Umm. Nothing. Just... yeah—the food looked different online."

"Do you..." She shot a look towards the images over the bar. "Do you want to get out of here? Maybe grab some cheap food at a drive through and go for a drive or something?"

He perked up.

"It's not that this place isn't lovely... Just..."

"It's not you," he said.

"I was going to say it's not *you,*" she countered, holding back a grin.

For a moment, the two of them studied each other, their minds cycling through the options of offense, amusement, awkward silence.

In the end, though, Ilse said. "I'm really glad we're doing this. I'm sorry I didn't say yes sooner."

Sawyer watched her. "What changed your mind?"

She looked determinedly away from the television. She met his gaze. Then said simply, "I like being around you more than I like being away from you."

He considered this. Then tapped his nose. "You think I'm hot. I knew it."

She snorted but Sawyer was pushing to his feet, grabbing his jacket. He tossed a twenty on the table. "Should cover the reservation," he muttered. "Let's get out of here. Thank God. I wasn't sure I could stay seated back there much longer."

Ilse couldn't resist smiling now as Sawyer looped his arm through hers and began leading back towards the doors.

It was the shortest date she'd ever been on. At least... the shortest meal... Then again, it was the only date she'd ever *really* been on. She kept shooting glances towards Tom, making sure he was still smiling. Even when he wasn't, though, his eyes carried mirth. Carried joy.

She'd never seen him so happy before.

She supposed he was really excited for a burger. Or maybe... she shifted her injured arm, and allowed him to lead her by her other hand out through the door, into the night.

Maybe she'd made the right call returning.

Sometimes, she realized, she spent so much time dwelling on old memories, she forgot to make new ones.

As Sawyer began chatting cheerfully about some new project of his in the garage, involving wood and drills and glues and all manner of things that carried no interest to Ilse, she was determined not to miss a moment. Not on past memories. Not on future dreams.

But on the very real, and very happy present.

A NEW SERIES!

NOW AVAILABLE!

<u>WITHOUT MERCY</u>

(A Dakota Steele FBI Suspense Thriller—Book 1)

MMA champ-turned-FBI Special Agent and BAU specialist Dakota Steele is as tough as they come—and as brilliant, too, able to crack serial killers that no one else can. But this new case is unlike anything she's seen, and Dakota, weighed down by the demons of her own past, may have just reached her breaking point.

"The plot has many twists and turns, but it is the ending, which I did not see coming at all, that totally defines this book as one of the most riveting that I have read in years."
—Reader review for Not Like Us

WITHOUT MERCY is the debut novel of a brand new series by critically-acclaimed and #1 bestselling mystery and suspense author Ava Strong.

Dakota's last case broke her, driving her to quit the FBI and return to the hard streets of her South Dakota hometown. She is weighed down by a lifetime of fighting, and by the demons of her dark past: her missing sister who vanished when Dakota was a teenager. Her estranged father, who she still can't bring herself to speak to.

The killer she let get away.

Dakota has hit her low point.

Only the most desperate case—and the tough love of her partner—can lure her back.

Victims are disappearing along empty stretches of desert highway, with no witnesses. The landscape is desolate, the people tough and dangerous. And the police are stumped.

Time is running out before the next victim is taken, and it's up to Dakota to connect the dots.

Can Dakota stop him in time?

Or will her own demons take her for good?

A complex psychological crime thriller full of twists and turns and packed with heart-pounding suspense, the DAKOTA STEELE mystery series will make you fall in love with a brilliant new female protagonist and keep you turning pages late into the night.

Books #2 and #3 in the series—WITHOUT REMORSE and WITHOUT A PAST—are now also available.

Ava Strong

Bestselling author Ava Strong is author of the REMI LAURENT mystery series, comprising six books (and counting); of the ILSE BECK mystery series, comprising seven books (and counting); of the STELLA FALL psychological suspense thriller series, comprising six books (and counting); and of the DAKOTA STEELE FBI suspense thriller series, comprising three books (and counting).

An avid reader and lifelong fan of the mystery and thriller genres, Ava loves to hear from you, so please feel free to visit www.avastrongauthor.com to learn more and stay in touch.

BOOKS BY AVA STRONG

REMI LAURENT FBI SUSPENSE THRILLER
THE DEATH CODE (Book #1)
THE MURDER CODE (Book #2)
THE MALICE CODE (Book #3)
THE VENGEANCE CODE (Book #4)
THE DECEPTION CODE (Book #5)
THE SEDUCTION CODE (Book #6)

ILSE BECK FBI SUSPENSE THRILLER
NOT LIKE US (Book #1)
NOT LIKE HE SEEMED (Book #2)
NOT LIKE YESTERDAY (Book #3)
NOT LIKE THIS (Book #4)
NOT LIKE SHE THOUGHT (Book #5)
NOT LIKE BEFORE (Book #6)
NOT LIKE NORMAL (Book #7)

STELLA FALL PSYCHOLOGICAL SUSPENSE THRILLER
HIS OTHER WIFE (Book #1)
HIS OTHER LIE (Book #2)
HIS OTHER SECRET (Book #3)
HIS OTHER MISTRESS (Book #4)
HIS OTHER LIFE (Book #5)
HIS OTHER TRUTH (Book #6)

DAKOTA STEELE FBI SUSPENSE THRILLER
WITHOUT MERCY (Book #1)
WITHOUT REMORSE (Book #2)
WITHOUT A PAST (Book #3)

www.ingramcontent.com/pod-product-compliance
Lightning Source LLC
Chambersburg PA
CBHW030615310726
48979CB00003B/732

* 9 7 8 1 0 9 4 3 9 5 4 0 1 *